Pete Johnson

Pete Johnson has been a film extra in flop films, an English teacher, and a film critic for Radio One. Yet his dream was always to be a writer.

When he was ten years old Pete wrote a fan letter to Dodie Smith, the author of his favourite book, *The Hundred and One Dalmatians*. His friends doubted that she would even bother to reply. In fact, Dodie Smith was to correspond with Pete for many years, and was the first to urge him to be a writer. Two of Pete's books are dedicated to her. Pete is also careful to answer all the fan letters he now receives each month.

Also in the Contents series

Also by Pete Johnson

Contents

The Vision

PETE JOHNSON

mammoth

First published in Great Britain in 1996 by Mammoth
an imprint of Reed International Books Ltd
Michelin House, 81 Fulham Road, London SW3 6RB
and Auckland, Melbourne, Singapore and Toronto

ISBN 0 7497 2663 6

10 9 8 7 6 5 4 3 2

A CIP catalogue record for this title is available
from the British Library

Typeset by Deltatype Ltd, Ellesmere Port, Cheshire
Printed in Great Britain by Cox & Wyman Ltd, Reading, Berkshire

This book is dedicated to Jan, Linda, Robin and Harry;
Tanya van Dissel; Daniel Phibbs; Bill Bloomfield;
Rose Jewitt; and to my editor, Miriam Hodgson, for
her endless understanding.

Contents

1 Revenge

She just wanted it to be over.

'We can wait if you . . .?' began Katie.

'No,' interrupted Tara. 'Come on.'

They walked quickly through the youth club: past the girls sitting on the sofa with the stuffing falling out; past the boys picking teams to play five-a-side football, and over to the pool table where the real men hung out, the ones who carried their motorbike helmets like trophies and spent all their money on a designer shirt. Only the elite could strut here.

And once Tara had been an honorary member. One night she'd been sitting on the sofa all dressed up, when Phil journeyed over from the pool table. All the girls were on full alert. But it was Tara those baby blue eyes sought out. Before he'd spoken she'd already fallen for him.

He introduced her to his mates, none of whom she knew as they went to Priestley High, the school on the other side of the village. By the end of the evening he'd asked her out and become her first serious boyfriend.

For eleven weeks and four days Phil took over her whole life.

Then, at the beginning of July – 8 July to be precise – she was dropped. Phil didn't actually tell her in person, he left that little task to one of his mates: the foxy-faced one she'd always disliked. His mate didn't offer Tara any explanation, save for a vague hint that she had become too clingy. He also informed her there was no point in seeking an appeal; Phil was, apparently, unavailable for further comment.

The rest of that night had a sick, dream-like quality. The rest of the summer, too. But she'd sorted herself out. She must keep reminding herself of that fact.

Phil was running his fingers through his long blond hair, and smiling to himself as he did so – something he often did. How could she ever have found that mannerism charming?

The pack gathered round Phil, staring curiously at the two gate-crashers. Attendance at this part of the youth club was strictly by invitation only. But Phil's eyes quickly passed over them. He seemed to be deep in thought.

Tara took two deep breaths. Her heart was beating furiously.

'Phil, I've got something of yours.'

He almost looked at her, but not quite, though it didn't much matter whether he looked at her or not. She reached inside her pocket.

'I've got something of yours,' she repeated. His face was as still as a stone. He didn't even raise an eyebrow. But she had the attention of his mates all right. And others, sensing a piece of drama, were edging forward, too. She faced her growing audience. 'I bet you didn't know Phil can't get to sleep without his little toy. Well, he can't and here's the proof.' Then, with the triumphant flourish of a conjuror about to dazzle, she produced a photograph of seventeen-year-old Phil tightly clutching a black and white seal.

As she waved the snapshot around Tara remembered when she'd discovered the seal on Phil's bed. At first he'd been highly embarrassed, finally he'd confided in her: he'd had that seal – old Sam as he called it – since he was a small boy. His mother had given it to him shortly before she walked out. Later, when he'd had to go to hospital to have his tonsils out, old Sam came too. And even now he couldn't relegate it to the attic.

At the time Tara had been touched by this glimpse of Phil's more vulnerable side. That's why she had wanted a picture of Phil hugging old Sam. After much persuasion he finally consented. 'I tell you, if anyone sees that I'm a dead man,' he'd said. She'd laughed and said she was going to send it to the local paper. He'd pretended to be worried then, said he'd have to destroy the camera, but really he trusted her. And she'd kept it hidden away in her drawer as he'd instructed. Even after he'd dumped her.

But then, last week she'd returned to the youth club for the first time in nearly two months. All summer she'd kept away; it was just too painful. But she'd heard on the grapevine that Phil was away on holiday. It seemed a good time to creep back. She had walked straight into an ambush. Phil's pack had started circling her and Katie. It was the foxy-looking one who began: 'That letter you wrote to Phil, it was so moving,' he sneered. And then, one by one, they began quoting lines from her letter, the one she'd written pleading with Phil not to leave her. Actually, they only managed to speak three or four words before breaking out into laughter. But the quotes were accurate enough. It was a corny, deeply embarrassing letter, one she should have written and then buried away in a drawer, just as Katie had advised. Only she hadn't. Somehow, she'd believed her sad desperate words would send Phil hurtling back. Instead . . . instead he'd passed it among his cronies and indeed – as a girl from her class later confirmed – around the whole youth club. At first all she could feel was a terrible, crushing shame. But later his cruelty, his act of betrayal, made her so angry that all she could think about was doing something to even the score.

Tonight she'd done just that. All around Phil was loud, derisive laughter. Not only at the toy seal but at that silly, rapt look he'd adopted. He'd just been messing about, of course, but it made the photo even more incriminating.

Suddenly Phil made a grab for the photo. Tara was too quick

4

though; she snatched it away from him, calling out, 'Anyone else want to see Phil and his favourite toy?' By his one action Phil had greatly increased the photo's value. Everyone had to see it now.

'I think we should get some copies done,' cried Katie, 'stick them around the place.'

'What a great idea,' shouted Tara.

Phil's pack were becoming alarmed by all this mockery. They turned on him: 'What were you doing?' the foxy-faced one asked him. 'You looked a right prat.' He sounded indignant, bewildered. Phil didn't answer. Instead, just for a moment he caught Tara's eye. He looked stunned, as if he couldn't quite believe the extent of her treachery. How dare he look at her like that, thought Tara. After all he'd put her through. How dare he.

'Give me that picture,' he muttered. It was both a command and a plea.

'Only when I get my letter back,' she hissed.

He didn't reply. Instead, he shot past her and out of the youth club. Tara stared after him for a moment, then put the photo away. 'You certainly showed him,' cried a girl from her class. Phil's mates went into a huddle.

Tara didn't want to stay any longer. Her mission had been accomplished. Even though it was drizzling with rain, she and Katie walked back up to the village talking and talking about what had happened.

'I just wanted him to know how it feels to be humiliated,' said Tara.

'He knows all right,' said Katie.

'And now he'll see I've got the strength to . . . he'd better give me my letter back, that's all.' She stifled a yawn. At first she'd been elated, triumphant; now she just wanted to crawl into bed.

'Would you mind if I don't go round to Matt's with you?' asked Tara. Matt was Tara's other best friend. In a way she and Katie shared him. A friendship *à trois*, as Katie once dubbed it.

'Oh, why not?'

'I'm dead tired.'

'Well you can crash out at Matt's. He won't mind,' cried Katie. 'Come on, you don't want to go home now on your night of triumph.'

'Yes I do,' said Tara quietly.

They stood outside Tara's house.

'You are a let-down,' said Katie.

'I know.'

'No, you were brilliant tonight. Deadly, but cool.'

'And for once my eyes didn't wobble at all?' asked Tara

'No, you didn't do anything embarrassing. Like I said, you were brilliant. Mind you, after what he put you through you should have broken his legs . . . I'm just so happy it's all over.'

'Not as happy as me,' said Tara. 'I can't believe I let him take me over like that.'

'You were in *lurve*.'

'Never again.'

'Fourteen and finished with love,' said Katie. She smiled disbelievingly.

'No, honestly, I'm not letting anyone get to me like that again . . . I'm free now and that's the way I want to stay.'

'I believe you,' said Katie in a voice which suggested the opposite. Tara grinned at her. Everyone said Katie had a very cheeky face; she was someone you felt at ease with instantly. And boys were interested in Katie. Tara kept telling her that, but somehow Katie never had much confidence in herself. Recently, at a party, a boy had bumped into her and said, 'Hey, I wouldn't want to get into a fight with you. You're solid.' She at once made a joke of it, but Tara knew that silly – and very unfair – comments like that stabbed Katie deeply.

'It's just such a shame this had happened when there's no summer holiday left,' began Katie. She stopped, and then cried, 'Look.'

'What?'

'There's a lime-green Beetle in your drive.' Katie and Tara looked at each other and remembered.

'Oh no,' cried Tara, 'I'd forgotten all about him.'

Tonight her home was being invaded. Her dad was temporarily unemployed, as her nan put it, so he was unable to send them as much money as he'd have liked. He'd have a new job soon, of course, but until then her grandparents just had their small pension and savings, and as her dad never used the third bedroom now, it made sense to rent it out.

When they'd first mentioned this plan Tara had just nodded guiltily, mumbling something about getting a Saturday job. But her grandparents had brushed that aside; this was only a temporary cash-flow problem which a lodger would help them solve.

But Nan was quite fussy about who this lodger should be: 'You hear such funny stories,' she said. It wasn't until she met the headmaster of Tara's school at the PTA dinner and dance that a solution was reached. There was a new English and PE teacher starting at the school in September and he was looking for somewhere to stay. Nan was immediately hooked: a teacher, well that was all right, bound to be someone very respectable and clean.

Nan and Grandad told her the headmaster had promised this guy wouldn't actually teach Tara, but still they realised it could be rather strange having a teacher from her school also living in her house. . . . It was only now with her mind clear again that it really hit Tara.

They walked around his car, peering into every window. 'Look at all those papers on the back seat, that's a teacher's car all right,' said Katie. 'I bet it smells as if dogs have been in there. Teachers' cars always smell of dogs,' she grinned. 'Now I know why you were rushing home. You just can't wait to meet the new man in your life.'

'How did you guess? It's going to be gruesome, isn't it?'

'No, it'll be lovely,' she giggled. 'First thing in the morning as you're stumbling along to the bathroom, who will you bump into, but your teacher?'

'He won't be *my* teacher.'

'Oh yes he will,' teased Katie. 'I'm sure he'll check you do your homework at night . . . maybe he'll be like Mr Toms and have sweaty armpits, and he won't do his shirt up properly so his belly button hangs out.'

They were both laughing now.

'It's going to be so gross,' said Tara.

'All right, it will be and he's in your house waiting for you right now.'

'Oh, I'm going straight to bed,' murmured Tara.

'I bet you get called down to say hello,' said Katie.

'I'll just pretend I can't hear.'

Tara opened the door and pushed her way through the curtain which, to her friends' great amusement, Nan kept in front of the door to keep the draughts out. She really didn't want to be introduced to this new lodger tonight. She decided to make a run for it.

She was fast but she wasn't fast enough.

2 The power returns to Tara

Just as Tara reached the top of the stairs her nan called up, 'Tara, dear, don't go up those stairs two at a time, I think that's what's making them creak.'

'Yes, all right Nan,' she said impatiently.

'It's not your fault dear, this house isn't built very well.'

'That's true,' she replied, not really listening. 'Anyway, night.'

'Tara!' cried her nan and she sounded so shocked Tara turned round.

'But he's here, he's arrived.' Nan was acting as if the New Messiah was in the dining-room.

'I'm feeling a bit tired . . .' Tara began.

Nan's voice rose indignantly. 'First your grandfather says he can't cancel his train night, so he's up there,' she pointed to the loft, 'playing trains with the other elderly schoolboys and may as well not be here at all, but I thought I could rely on you for some support. But no, everything's just left to me, as usual.'

Tara knew when she was beaten. 'I'll just say hello.' She trudged down the stairs again.

Nan was beaming now. She was small with short grey hair, pink cheeks and very bright blue eyes. In the house she always wore a pale blue overall which Tara thought made her look like a shop assistant.

'Now speak nice and loud, Tara. What you've got to say is worth hearing, it's just a shame people can't always hear it.'

When she was younger Tara had been very shy, now she spoke up. But her nan didn't seem to have caught up with these changes; no wonder sometimes Tara felt as if she was living in a time warp.

Nan opened the dining-room door, and then, as an afterthought, knocked.

'Mr Martin, this is my granddaughter, Tara. She wanted to say hello.' A figure got up from the green armchair they'd brought down from the loft. He was dark-skinned, tall – very tall – quite muscular and young. His hair was thick and glossy.

'Please call me Paul,' he said, stretching out a hand to Tara. Then he smiled at her and it was such an open, friendly smile it was almost shocking.

He was wearing a white shirt and jeans with a smart waistcoat. He was, Tara conceded, quite good-looking. She was certain girls in her class would like him.

At least her lodger wasn't a total idiot. She felt a little stab of pride about that. But then, as her eyes travelled around the room, she couldn't help noticing how cluttered it was: there was the heavy oak dining-room table and chairs, a desk, a china cabinet, two more chairs and a footstool. There was enough furniture in here for two or three rooms. But it wasn't only crowded, it was also unbelievably tasteless thanks to her nan's mania for sticking frills over everything she could find – chair covers, cushions, pelmets (nothing escaped) – and all those rows of cheap-looking china shoes, not to mention a mantlepiece crowded with deeply embarrassing family photos.

But she'd stopped noticing it, until this stranger turned up and made her feel all self-conscious. She wondered what he was really thinking about this house, and Nan, and herself. Inside was he sniggering?

Nan was twittering on: 'And do you know, Tara, this poor man hasn't eaten all day.'

'Your nan's spoiling me,' grinned Paul.

'Well, we can't have you passing out with hunger on your first day, can we?' said Nan.

Tara noticed, beside his chair, the book he'd been reading when they came in. It was unmistakable: the Bible.

'Our school's not that bad,' said Tara, nodding at the Bible. 'Praying for help, were you?'

His deep brown eyes glinted with amusement. 'Think I'll need it, do you?'

She smiled back. 'Tell you tomorrow.' She wondered why he was reading the Bible. Probably for a lesson he was preparing. That didn't sound very promising. Still, he seemed a bit of a laugh.

'Now, don't you worry, Paul,' broke in Nan. 'It's a nice school; I know the headmaster personally. It's quite small, so of course they've been trying to close it for years. Can't leave anything alone, can they? But we sent them a petition, wrote letters to the local press, even had stickers on the back of our cars, so I think that's an end to that . . . Why, Tara's father went to that school,' she added, as if that was another major reason for keeping it open.

The door opened and Grandad peered round. 'We're just off for a swift half.'

'Yes, well, off you go then. Have a nice time,' said Nan, in distinctly huffy tones.

Grandad edged inside, grinned faintly at his new lodger, then tapped Tara on the shoulder. 'This was on the mat for you.' He handed her a letter. 'Delivered by hand too,' he winked at Tara. 'Bound to be a love letter, then.'

Her grandad was right. It was a love letter. Upstairs, in the privacy of her room, Tara ran her eye over a few of the choicest phrases. How about, 'You found the secret passageway into my heart.' She shuddered. Had she really written this mush? She glanced at the last line. 'Whatever you decide, please contact me, even if it's just for five minutes. Please.' Of course nothing she did had stirred him into action. Not until tonight when his own ego, his precious status with his mates, had been threatened. He must have run straight home.

So at last she'd given him some pain back. Tara gloated about this for a moment. The power was with her, not Phil any more.

Phil. There was nothing to him really. You could put your hand straight through him. But for a while, she'd gazed at him through a romantic mist and seen so many wonderful things. Now the mist had lifted and he'd just disappeared. Like this letter was about to.

Tara tore it into tinier and tinier pieces. 'Ashes to ashes,' she whispered. Then she put the photo of him and old Sam into an envelope. She'd keep her part of the bargain; tomorrow she'd post it back to him, second class.

She got up and stared outside. The rain was pattering against the glass. But there were no stars, nothing but darkness pressing against the window. In the past, this was when she'd snuggle into bed and start to lose herself in a book. One wall of her bedroom was completely covered with books as she could never bear to throw any away. It was almost as if her whole life was on that wall: all those picture books Nan had bought her, the sets of Narnia, E. Nesbit, Roald Dahl, her beloved *One Hundred and One Dalmatians*, then all the horsey books, followed by tales of mystery and horror.

On a shelf, all by itself, were her special favourites: the Jennings books. These had belonged to her dad, and they were quite old even when he'd read them. Big, fat hardbacks, all featuring grinning schoolboys in purple caps and blazers encountering bewildered-looking adults. Tara must have been nine or ten when she found them one night by the light of the torch which her grandparents had given her, in case she ever woke up in the dark and felt afraid. She devoured three of them, one after the other. Linbury Court always seemed much friendlier and happier and much more real, somehow, than her middle school.

After she started at Rayner School and met Katie, her social life improved dramatically, but there were still times when she revisited the Jennings books. She would always be grateful to them; they'd helped her get through a lonely, miserable time.

Nan told her once that the Jennings books were her dad's favourites too. It was one of the very few times she'd felt close to him.

She still loved books. But since she'd met Phil she hadn't been able to lose herself in stories the way she used to. Her old life had gone. And she was in this strange kind of limbo, just drifting, not really anywhere. And all because of Phil.

She thought again of what she'd done tonight. There could be no reconciliation now. That tiny whisper of hope had finally been buried deep in the ground where it should have been buried long before this. But it still felt a bit scary, a bit strange. Now it was official, she was living in a Phil-less universe.

3 Paul's
apple girl

'Another term in that hell-hole,' said Katie, gloomily.

Tara nodded. Although she knew, as schools went, Rayner wasn't so bad. It was very old and from the outside looked quite impressive: big iron gates with the school coat of arms on them, brick walls covered with ivy and massive great playing-fields. Yet, inside, the school had a shabby, neglected air. The classrooms were often freezing (the heaters only seemed to blow out cold air), and, when it was wet, the rain could be heard rhythmically drumming into hastily positioned buckets.

Leaning by the school gate was Matt in his uniform: farmer's cap back to front, shirt already hanging out, big white trainers and a green anorak. Anoraks were not exactly high fashion at Rayner; that was why Matt delighted in wearing one. Tara couldn't help envying Matt's total lack of interest in looking trendy. In fact, he tried so hard not to be cool he was cool.

In one hand Matt was brandishing a Mars bar, in the other a can of Coke. He waved them both at Tara and Katie.

Katie rubbed her eyes disbelievingly. 'I can't believe it, this is all a dream. You're never here before midday.'

'It's my mum's fault. I think she's had some kind of brainstorm. She came shrieking into my room at seven o'clock – *seven o'clock*! – like some demented banshee shrieking some nonsense that now I'm starting GCSEs I should turn over a new leaf and get to school on time . . . "You'll never do as well as your brothers, you know," ' he mimicked. Matt had two older brothers, both at university now.

Katie gazed at him quizzically. 'Just out of interest, do you ever do things like . . . brush your hair?'

'That's a very personal question. And I'll have to consult my lawyer before I say any more.' He put the rest of the Mars bar into his mouth. 'Just thought I'd finish it before either of you asked me for some.'

'Generous to a fault that boy,' said Tara. 'I'm sorry I couldn't come round last night.'

'So you should be. Hope you've brought a note. Last night . . . it went all right then?' Suddenly, he looked awkward. Tara felt awkward too.

A few months ago she would have said it was impossible to have an argument with Matt. He was never serious enough, but, after she'd started seeing Phil, Matt had made a rare visit to the youth club to meet this 'paragon of perfection'. Matt just saw Phil in the distance but immediately criticised him. He believed Phil was one of those guys who thinks everyone should bow down to him, and he'd soon start messing Tara around. In the end he got Tara so mad she stormed off.

Phil hadn't been especially impressed by Matt either. He couldn't understand that Matt was a very good friend, not a prospective boy-friend.

Tara hardly spoke to Matt for weeks. Then, after she'd been chucked, Matt came round. He never once said, 'I told you so,' he never mentioned Phil directly at all. He acted as if she'd been very ill and was now convalescing.

'Yes, last night went fine,' said Tara.

'She was brilliant,' said Katie. 'Really socked it to him.'

'Excellent, excellent . . . Just saw Big Hands Purvey drive in.'

'And has he still got his lovely ginger sideburns?' asked Tara, as eager as Matt to move on to another subject.

'They're more wonderful than ever,' he replied. 'And Commissioner Gordon's just steamed past as well.' The headmaster was, according to Matt, a dead ringer for Commissioner Gordon, the character from the *Batman* TV series. He also claimed that the headmaster had a red Bat-phone in his office, though only Matt had ever spotted this.

'But what I want to know about,' said Matt, 'is the geek who's staying with you.'

'He's not a geek,' said Tara quickly. 'As I said to Katie, he's . . .'

'He told her to call him Paul,' interrupted Katie.

'Ho, ho,' said Matt.

'No, he's . . . that's him,' she cried, for at that moment Paul drove past. He saw Tara, grinned and waved exuberantly, as if he were setting off on his holidays.

'He's a bit happy, isn't he?' said Matt.

'He was all smiles at breakfast as well,' replied Tara.

'If there's one thing I hate, it's really happy teachers. It's not natural,' Matt went on.

'He looks quite fit though, doesn't he?' said Katie.

Matt turned to Tara. 'Fancy him, do you?'

'Oh yeah, I think he's so lovely,' replied Tara, in her soppiest voice.

'And I bet you get asked about him all day,' said Katie.

Katie was right. All the girls in Tara's year were just buzzing with interest. By far the most popular question was 'Has he got a girlfriend?'

'Now how do I know?' exclaimed Tara. 'I'm not exactly going to go up and ask him, am I?'

But in fact when she arrived home that evening her nan was hissing at her in the hallway.

'I've just spoken to Paul's lady friend, Clare. She rang here,' she added.

'I guessed that, Nan. So what did she want?'

'She wanted Paul to ring her as soon as he got in, sounded quite . . .' Nan searched for the right word, '. . . quite distraught. What on earth do you think can have happened?'

'Maybe she's pregnant,' said Tara.

'Oh my goodness. Do you think so?'

'Could be. After all, we don't really know anything about him, do we?' Tara was being mischievous. Her nan got wound up very easily. 'Or maybe he's run off with all her savings.'

'Now you're being silly. I'd know if he was up to anything like that.'

'How would you know?'

'That's him,' hissed Nan.

'No earwigging when he's on the phone, Nan,' Tara teased.

'Of course we must let him have his privacy,' said Nan.

A key turned in the lock. But it wasn't Paul who appeared, it was Tara's dad. Nan rushed over to him beaming with pleasure. 'This is a surprise. You never said anything last night.'

'No, well I found myself in the area, seeing a few contacts so . . .' he breezed over to Tara, kissing her somewhat awkwardly on the top of her head. 'How's my girl?'

'My girl.' That's what Phil used to call her. How easily that phrase tripped off their tongues. It meant absolutely nothing.

She didn't bother to reply.

'We thought you were Paul, our new lodger,' said Nan.

'Arrived, has he?' asked her dad a little too casually. 'What's he like?'

'Very nice,' replied Nan. 'Young, still needs looking after, I think.' She said this quite fondly. 'We've given him the dining-room as well as his bedroom.'

Tara's dad immediately walked into the dining-room and looked around. 'New chair,' he said, pointing at the green chair in the corner.

'Yes, we brought that down for Paul, so if he has a friend over and they don't want to sit at the table . . . he had a call actually, from a young lady. She sounded quite anxious for him to ring her.'

Tara's dad tut-tutted. 'I hope he's not going to start any of that.'

'Any of what?' cried Tara. 'He's entitled to have phone calls, isn't he?'

'Of course he is,' replied her dad. 'It's just a bit rich having them so soon. Don't have any nonsense from him. If there's anything you're unhappy about, tell him right away.'

'Oh, there's nothing,' said Nan, 'except for – well – when I went into the bathroom this morning his aftershave caught in my throat. I was going to ask him if he'd use a little less or use it in his room. And if he would take his shoes off in the house it would save my poor old carpets.'

'Nan, you can't start saying things like that to him,' said Tara. 'You'll give him a complex. He'll be afraid to breathe next.'

'If your nan merely points out . . .' began her dad.

'No,' cried Tara, stung into anger by her dad's attitude. He was trying to stir things up. 'No, you mustn't ever say that to him.' She glared at her dad. 'You're just being petty.'

Another key sounded in the lock. This time it was Paul. But if he was phased at finding them in his room, he didn't show it.

'Paul, this is my son, Stuart,' said Nan. As they shook hands Tara couldn't help noticing how much smaller her dad was than Paul. 'Well, we'll leave you in peace,' said Nan. Tara's dad was supposed to follow Nan into the sitting-room. Instead, he slowly walked over to the green chair and sat down. He grinned around at them. 'I'm gasping for a cup of tea.'

Tara watched this performance contemptuously. Now she knew why he was honouring them with his presence, he'd come to show the lodger that this was still his territory.

'I've got some things to do upstairs,' said Paul, tactfully. 'See you later then.'

'Stay and join us, if you like,' said Tara, 'this is your room anyway.'

Nan laughed embarrassedly. 'Yes, would you like a cup of tea, Paul?'

'Not just now, thanks.' Paul made as if to go, then Nan called after him.

'Oh, Paul, in all the excitement, I forgot to tell you, you had a phone call from Clare.'

Tara was almost certain his smile faded a little.

'She asked you to ring her right away. Said it was urgent,' continued Nan. 'So feel free to use the phone, it's in the hall.'

'Hidden under a pile of coats,' added Tara.

'Great, thanks a lot,' he said, closing the door behind him.

'Hope you're going to keep a record of all his calls,' said Dad, as soon as Paul had left.

'Oh, honestly, honestly,' cried Tara.

'Sssh,' warned Nan. They heard him pounding up the stairs. 'He's not going to ring her,' Nan sounded disappointed.

'Can you blame him,' said Tara, 'with us all listening?' She suddenly felt protective, as if it was up to her to look out for his rights.

'He could have chucked you out of here, you know. This is his room. He pays rent for it.'

'That's enough, Tara,' said Nan. 'Paul understands that he is living here as part of the family and sometimes . . . well your father's here now, so sit down and talk to him while I make us all a nice cup of tea.' She spoke gently but it was a command just the same. Tara reluctantly sat down opposite her dad. 'That's better,' said Nan, 'your grandad should be home soon.'

'Where's he gone?' asked Tara's dad.

'Oh he doesn't bother telling me things like that,' snapped Nan. She bustled out to the kitchen leaving Tara and her dad staring uncertainly at each other.

He'd definitely put on weight, Tara thought. He was getting quite fat. His suit was creased and rather shabby-looking, especially in comparison with the smart grey suit Paul was wearing today. Her dad had the air of someone who was going down in the world.

It was hard to believe that grinning, confident figure in the framed wedding photo was her father. She never remembered him being like that. And as for her mum . . . sometimes Tara would lie awake at night racing after a memory of her mum, but the memory would always elude her at the last moment. Tara had a horrible feeling that all she actually remembered was her mum's funeral. She was four and she kept asking over and over, 'But what does "died" mean?'

No one could make her understand until, finally, an elderly vicar sat her on his knee and explained: 'Our body is really like a parcel. At the moment all we see is what's outside, the wrapping. But when we

23

die we don't need the wrapping any more so we can throw it away. But what's inside us – which is what we really are – that goes on,' and he pointed upwards, 'to Heaven.'

Sometimes at night Tara would stare out of the window and think of her mum out there somewhere, soaring into space. But there were other times when her mum was just a black and white photograph on the bedside cabinet. It was taken just four days before the car accident, and there was already something other-worldly about her mum: those huge, doe eyes which took up most of her face, gazing into the distance.

Tara would stare and stare into that photograph and then peer at her own reflection, searching for similarities. She had the same long dark hair as her mum and similar eyes, too. Nan told her she was growing more and more like her mother. Tara hoped that was true. When she was younger she used to dream about her mum a lot. The dreams always started with her springing out of that picture frame and taking Tara by the hand. Often they'd end up on the beach where they'd just talk and talk.

'So, first day back at school,' said her dad with an awkward smile.

Tara stared coolly back at him.

'How did it go?'

'All right,' she muttered. Why should she make an effort to talk to him? He was only here because he was on some silly ego trip.

He went on, 'I remember the first day of term, you'd walk into school and there'd be this smell of polish everywhere. You couldn't

24

get away from it. I used to feel as if I was drowning in the stuff. I suppose they still have that?'

Tara shrugged her shoulders. 'Couldn't tell you.'

'And assembly. You must have had one of those awful school assemblies: everyone in the sports hall, no shoes allowed so you'd get this lovely smell of cheese everywhere.'

'We didn't have assembly today,' said Tara, curtly.

'Didn't have assembly . . . Rayner always has assembly on the first morning.'

'Didn't today,' replied Tara. She'd been rather surprised herself. But she wasn't going to admit it.

'Well, I don't know,' said her dad. 'There'll be questions in Parliament about that.' He was trying desperately to be funny, to make some contact with her. Tara would almost feel sorry for him, if he weren't her dad.

Instead, she watched him with growing resentment. Did he really think he could wander in here and start playing her dad again for ten minutes before shooting off for another six weeks? Maybe she should send him one of those stickers you see on car windows: A DOG'S NOT JUST FOR CHRISTMAS. IT'S FOR LIFE. Only she'd change 'DOG' into 'DAUGHTER'.

Where was he when she needed him? Where had he been on 8 July when Phil chucked her?

Her grandparents were there for her, of course. She hadn't told them about Phil at first. Then, on Saturday, Grandad drove her and Nan into town. They were in one of these carparks with about twenty

25

storeys and Grandad was trying to manoeuvre into a space when this huge car appeared out of nowhere, backed up right behind him and refused to move. Poor old Grandad was sweating, Nan was calling things out of the window and Tara suddenly burst into tears. 'Why are people so nasty?' she sobbed. And she couldn't stop crying.

Finally, Grandad drove back home again and she told them the whole story. 'I knew something was wrong,' exclaimed Nan, 'I knew it.' Then she and Grandad both became so anxious Tara felt guilty about telling them. Every time they asked her if she was feeling any better – about four times an hour – Tara pretended she was. It hadn't been fair to burden her grandparents. They'd done so much for her already. She had needed to talk to her dad. Nan said she'd told him and he was 'very concerned' – Nan always pretended her dad cared about her. *But he didn't do anything.*

'I just want you to know,' said her dad suddenly, 'that if you're not happy with this lodger . . .'

'His name's Paul,' said Tara sharply.

'Yes, well what I was trying to say, if you'll let me . . .' He's starting to get irritated now, thought Tara. At last she was getting to him. Good! 'If you're not happy about anything, Tara, we can sort something out. I should get another job soon and then I'll be able to . . . this is only a temporary measure.' He put on his understanding face. 'I certainly wouldn't have liked a teacher from my school knowing about me. We can have a re-think . . .'

'But I'm really pleased we have a lodger. And everyone at school is dead impressed. It's the best thing to have happened to me in years.' She stopped. Her dad was sinking down in his chair – correction, Paul's chair – now. The silence between them was vast, freezing. Finally, Tara got up and went out to the hall. She'd given him what he deserved; Phil last night, him today. Actually, Phil and her dad were quite similar. They could easily mess you up if you let them.

Nan called her back in for tea. Her dad hardly said another word; just gulped his down and left, bumping into Grandad at the door. Grandad sat down at the dining-room table reading the evening paper. Nan returned and started gathering up the cups. Tara sensed her nan wasn't happy.

'I heard what you said to your father, Tara . . . I think it upset him.'

'I'm so pleased,' said Tara bitterly.

'He's your father, Tara, and he loves you.'

'Oh yes, I can see that,' replied Tara, with undisguised irony.

Nan shook her head gravely. 'You know, when you were born your dad was the proudest person in the world. You – and your mother – meant everything to him. And when your mother was taken away, well, he just fell to pieces, went right back into his shell.'

Tara sighed impatiently. She'd heard all this many times before.

'No, you can make that face, but he still carries a picture of your mum in his breast pocket. She was his first girlfriend, you know.'

'You're just making excuses for him. He's a terrible father, and that's that.'

The tray in Nan's hand was shaking now. Grandad lowered his

paper. 'I think we've all said enough on this subject.' He had a habit of talking out of the side of his mouth, as if he were passing on secret information, but it gave a strange authority to his pronouncements.

Without another word Nan took the cups out to the kitchen. Tara hadn't meant to upset her. It was her dad . . . everything was his fault.

In the kitchen Nan could be heard banging the teacups on to the draining-board. Grandad slowly got up. At first Tara thought he was going out to Nan, instead he shuffled over to her, then asked: 'What's that behind your ear?' He reached forward and produced a five-pound note. It was an old party trick which her grandad had been performing for as long as she could remember.

'Go on, put it in your pocket. Don't leave money behind your ear, young Tara,' he said.

'Thanks, Grandad.'

His face, which could look grumpy and testy, relaxed into something much more genial. 'Don't thank me, it's magic.'

'Oh yes, I was forgetting, it's magic,' said Tara.

'How could you forget that?' Grandad shook his head for a moment in mock disgust. Then Paul appeared and Nan stopped attacking the teacups, and everyone plastered on smiles.

Later, Nan asked Paul whether he'd like to eat on his own or as part of the family: 'We won't be at all offended if you'd rather be left in peace,' said Nan. But then she smiled with relief when Paul said he'd love to eat with the family. They'd barely started eating when Nan was asking, 'Were you born in this country, dear?'

Tara shot her nan a look; this was so obviously nosy. But Paul didn't seem to mind. 'Yeah, I'm a Fulham boy. My parents were born in Trinidad, but they were students here when they had me so they fostered me out and saw me at weekends. We had some wonderful holidays in Trinidad, though, but after they split up I hardly saw them at all.'

'Oh dear,' murmured Nan.

'No, not really,' he said briskly, 'because then I went to live on this farm with Alan and Joyce, who were just brilliant. They had sixteen of us on that farm, gave us all jobs – my first one was feeding the chickens every day. I took it so seriously,' he grinned at the memory. 'Later on they taught me to ride. I had a great time. And they helped put me on the right road, because for a time I was a bit of a wild boy, or I thought I was anyhow. But don't worry, I'm a reformed character now,' he laughed so exuberantly it was hard not to join in.

'You've had some difficult times then, it hasn't been easy for you,' said Nan gently.

'I don't regret a second of my life,' replied Paul fervently. 'It's all helped to make me the person I am.'

'And you've done very well,' said Nan. 'Did you always want to be a teacher?'

'No, first of all I wanted to go into acting.' Tara could picture him as an actor, he had the energy and presence.

'But it didn't work out?' said Tara.

'Something like that. So I went on to the next best thing to acting, which is teaching and I'm really enjoying that. By the way, this chicken is delicious.'

'Yes, it is, isn't it?' said Nan, who, to Tara's embarrassment was never the least bit modest about her cooking. 'Got room for seconds, Paul?'

'And thirds,' he grinned.

Nan glowed with pleasure. 'It's nice to cook for someone who appreciates it,' she said, with a glance at Tara and her grandad who were picking at their meals.

Later that night Paul said he was going out for a breath of fresh air. Tara wondered if he was off to ring Clare in privacy. Maybe yesterday he'd had a blazing row with this Clare just before he'd left, and now she wanted to make up . . . Maybe. Different scenes kept playing around in Tara's head.

She'd only meant to tell Katie about Clare ringing. Now all the girls in her year were desperate for more details: was he still seeing her? He could be, was the frustratingly vague answer. He went out in his car some nights and most Sundays. But he never mentioned her.

Tara didn't tell anyone about Paul's early life, though. She felt that was too personal, somehow. It would have made her feel disloyal to gossip about him growing up in foster homes, even to Katie. Still, most mealtimes Tara discovered some snippet about Paul which she could pass on the next day: his favourite bands were Blur, Oasis and Madness; his top TV programme was *Fawlty Towers*; favourite actress was Michelle Pfeiffer.

Matt, of course, sent her up something rotten: 'Here she is, teacher's pet.'

'Don't you dare call me that,' cried Tara.

'OK, I'm sorry, apple girl.'

Tara had to smile. 'All right, I won't tell you the latest hot gossip then.'

'Let me guess,' said Matt. 'He has one sugar in his tea, but one and a half sugars in his coffee, except on Sunday when he goes a little crazy and has *two* sugars in his tea *and* coffee.'

'No,' said Katie, 'this is what happened: Tara was sitting in the lounge when Paul burst in and told her he couldn't hide his feelings for her any longer; he loves her madly. That's why he chucked Clare. When he saw Tara she wiped every other girl from his mind. That's right, isn't it Tara?'

'Oh, absolutely,' cried Tara. 'But I told him I didn't want to go out with anyone ever again.'

'Reckon you would say that, apple girl?' said Matt.

It was all fantasy, of course, but Tara had to admit she didn't mind all this attention. When she'd told her dad that having a lodger was one of the best things that had ever happened to her she'd only said it to taunt him. But now it was coming true.

For . . . whenever they had events at the school she always felt a bit ashamed, to be honest. Not that there was anything wrong with her grandparents; her friends always said how nice they were (and they were, they really were). But when she saw other people's parents and compared them with Nan in one of her flowery, Crimplene dresses, with the belt done up too tight so all her rolls of fat showed, carrying her white handbag, four times the size of anyone else's, and with

Grandad beside her in one of his sad blazers, she did wish there was someone else to represent her.

In a way, there was, now.

And it was all going so well until Paul just blew everything.

4 One of the God squad

It was a Friday morning and it was year ten assembly or, as Matt put it, 'Twenty minutes extra sleep.' Often, Miss Baker, the formidable deputy head would start the day with another rousing talk about litter. But today Paul joined her on the platform.

Katie whispered to Tara, 'Did you know he was doing this?'

'Hadn't a clue,' she replied.

'And we thought he told you everything,' said Matt.

Paul walked forward carrying a large envelope. He took a

photograph out of the envelope. Then he held it up, so that everyone could see it. It was a picture of him with his arms round a girl.

At once there were wolf whistles and cries of, 'Cor,' until Miss Baker stood up.

'I wonder if that's Clare?' hissed Katie.

'Yes folks, that wildly good-looking guy is me at the age of sweet sixteen,' Paul grinned cheekily, 'and with me is Lisa, who was my girlfriend at the time.'

'So she's not Clare?' exclaimed Katie.

'Who cares?' said Matt.

Paul went on: 'When I was sixteen I thought I was a pretty lucky guy. Apart from a nice girlfriend, I had good foster-parents . . .'

'Foster-parents. Did you know that?' Katie asked Tara.

Tara shook her head vaguely.

Paul continued: '. . . a pool of friends who'd always back me up in a fight. And I got into a few fights, but really, I was quite a placid, happy-go-lucky person. I'd go out raving from time to time but I learnt to keep my head down.'

Tara gazed around her. There had been little ripples when Paul mentioned fights and raving but everyone was listening intently to him. He wasn't talking assembly-speak. Tara couldn't help feeling a burst of pride in him.

'So, as I said, I was a pretty lucky guy. I had most of the things that are supposed to matter and yet there was something missing . . .'

'Tara was missing,' whispered Katie. Tara smiled but said nothing. Her heart was beating furiously, for some reason.

'You could say my life was a bit like a polo. There was all this stuff round the edges but right in the centre of my life there was this great hole. And while the stuff on the edges seemed to satisfy me for a while, I kept getting restless. Something was missing.' Matt whispered to Tara but she didn't catch it, she was too enthralled by Paul.

'What was missing? I tried lots of things, like going out with my mates all night, getting slaughtered, even drugs, very briefly.' Out of the corner of her eye Tara could see Miss Baker twitching in her chair. 'But none of those things filled the hole inside me,' he paused.

'And then I discovered the love of a good donkey,' whispered Matt. Both Tara and Katie shushed him.

'And then one day I was walking home, the same route I'd used every single day. And there was the church I'd passed every day for the past four years, with a cross in the window . . . that afternoon I turned and looked at the cross. I mean, *really* looked at it. I don't know why. I wasn't thinking about God or religion or anything. Far from it. But that day I saw the cross and then it was like someone turning a switch inside my head. All at once I saw how powerful that cross was. It reached inside me.

'After this I did something which might sound a bit weird: I started to laugh nervously. I was confused and excited. I'd spent all this time looking for something and here it was, right in front of me all the time. I'd just never seen it before. I knew then I'd made the most amazing discovery of my life.'

'He's one of the God squad,' cried Matt. There were similar groans all around Tara. She looked at Paul disbelievingly. His assembly was going really well until he threw it all away with this stuff about God.

'I'm not going to tell you any more,' said Paul.

'Good,' said Matt.

'But I'm running a Christian Union get-together next Tuesday. It's for everyone, not only Christians but anyone who is just looking and would like to hear more.'

'I reckon we'll all be going to that,' said Matt, contemptuously.

As the classes filed out a girl rushed over to Tara. 'I've gone right off him now,' she said, and then rushed off again.

Katie shook her head sadly. 'I really wish he hadn't done that assembly.'

'You're going to have to be careful,' said Matt. 'They never miss a chance to start preaching to you. I mean, if you say to him, "Have you seen my wallet?" he'll go,' Matt started talking in a high-pitched vicar's voice, ' "But don't you know, my child, money is the root of all evil." '

'He doesn't talk like that,' said Katie.

'No, but he'll bring God into everything. You'll see.'

'Look,' cried Tara, suddenly. 'So what if he is one of the God squad? So what?' But she didn't even convince herself. She couldn't help feeling that he'd let her down.

All morning Paul's assembly was a major talking point. People would come up to Tara and ask what it was like living with Jesus. Despite her disappointment in him, Tara found herself defending Paul and his right to be whatever he wanted.

But then, in the afternoon, came a new and even bigger sensation.

5 Rescue Rayner

After lunch normal lessons were cancelled. Instead there was to be an emergency assembly.

'Great, we'll miss maths,' cried Katie.

But a chill ran through Tara. She had a horrible feeling she knew what this assembly was about.

For once there was no teacher standing at the door to check everyone had taken their shoes off. Neither was there Miss Baker ordering everyone to 'fill up from the front, not the back'. This gave the whole event an oddly informal, end-of-term feel. The noise level was much higher than usual, too.

'There goes Jesus,' said Matt, as Paul took his place along the side of the room.

'We've had that joke,' said Tara, wearily. She couldn't help taking these comments personally.

Then all the talking fell away as the headmaster made his entrance. Unlike lesser mortals, he never asked for silence; he took that for granted.

Like his famous double, the headmaster had gleaming silver hair and a grave manner. There were rumours that he'd once been in the SAS bomb disposal unit, but no one had ever dared ask him. For, while he could be all right and even cracked the odd joke at Christmas, his death-stare could, as Matt observed, stop a werewolf in its tracks.

As Commissioner Gordon started to speak, Tara's worst fears were confirmed. 'I'm sorry to give you this bad news,' he said. 'But the county council has informed me that because of falling numbers our school is going to transfer to Priestley High next September.'

The school had been threatened with closure before and the council had deliberately created uncertainty, which meant parents sent their children to other, safer schools. Now the council could say the school had to close next summer because of falling numbers. Only they didn't use the word 'close', they said Rayner School would 'transfer' to Priestley High.

'How can you transfer a whole school?' said Katie, bitterly.

Commissioner Gordon read out some other stuff from the council, about how everyone would be given free bus passes and could still wear their old school uniform. Then he put the letter down, wrinkling his nose in disgust as he did so. 'That's what the council says. It thinks this school is beaten.' He paused for a moment. 'But I don't. That's why we're holding a meeting here on Monday night. We're going to invite the local press and Mr Martin has a contact in local television.' At once everyone's eyes fixed on Paul. 'So we're hoping to get them involved too.' This would send Paul's rating back up again. 'But,' the headmaster continued, 'we need every one of you here. We need everyone in your family here. And we need all our friends in the village here. That means sending out newsletters to every single household. Do we have any volunteers?'

Hands shot up all over the hall. Commissioner Gordon smiled his wintry smile.

'Thank you,' he murmured.

He left while form teachers rushed about taking the names of volunteers, and newsletters were passed from row to row.

At the top of the newsletter were two words: RESCUE RAYNER.

'This is so awful,' cried Katie, 'I mean, we've been through all this before. I thought they'd leave us alone now. Can you imagine having to go to Priestley? The sheer indignity of it all.'

'Priestley will have a field day,' said Tara. As she spoke she could picture the refugees from Rayner in their alien uniforms crawling into Priestley High, surrounded on all sides by jeers and taunts. She turned to Matt. 'You're very quiet. What have you got to say about all this?'

'If ever we needed the Caped Crusader, it's now,' said Matt. It was then Paul walked past and he smiled at Tara – just for a second – Matt and Katie missed it, but it was such an open, sympathetic smile she had no option but to smile back.

It wasn't the first time he'd smiled at her like that. At mealtimes her grandparents could act a bit funny with each other. They'd say things which seemed harmless enough but obviously had several layers of meaning for them. It was like they were playing some kind of private game and playing it so intently they forgot about everything else.

In the past when this happened Tara would just stare into her soup or something. Now that Paul was there too, well, at first, it was just very embarrassing. Then one day she caught his eye and they exchanged quick smiles. After that it was like a little secret between them. Tara wasn't on her own any more. He was in this with her; they were allies.

Tara turned her attention back to Matt who was saying, 'I think we three should just bombard the village with leaflets.' And that's what they did. They ended up leafletting the entire village. Other pupils must have had the same idea, because soon locals were complaining about the number of leaflets that were pouring through their letterboxes. Tara's grandad piled them all up on the kitchen table. 'Enough here to build a small mountain,' he grinned.

But it seemed to work because the meeting was packed out on Monday night. The pupils sat on benches and mats at the back of the hall while the rows of chairs were left for the adults. Soon, only the front row, which was left for all the councillors, was empty. More and more chairs had to be brought into the hall and still there weren't enough.

Finally, all the teachers vacated their seats and joined the pupils at the back.

Tara looked around her. There was a real buzz of anticipation tonight; just like the kind you get when concerts are about to start. Miss Baker was clearly the warm-up band, speaking very briefly through a microphone which kept cutting out. During her speech Tara's dad appeared, squeezing his way through to the seat her grandparents had saved for him. Trust him to be late. Still, Tara was surprised he was here at all. She was glad she was sitting far away from him. She saw him turn around, searching for her, but she deliberately kept her eyes fixed on the ground.

A tiny first-year boy got up, walked to the front of the hall and squeaked, 'Rayner can't close. I've only just got here.' There was laughter at this, but then the boy added solemnly, 'Rayner is my school and it's not going to close.' A man, immediately identifiable as his dad joined him. He put his hand on the boy's shoulder and declared, 'Rayner is my school and it's not going to close.' An elderly man was then helped to the front. He put his hand on the man's shoulder and with surprising force cried, 'Rayner is my school and it's not going to close.'

The three generations stood together, united, while the applause rained down on them. As they left the stage Paul bounded up to congratulate them. Then he led them outside to be filmed by the TV crew whom he'd managed to get to the meeting.

More and more people stood up to testify for Rayner School, then, to a huge roar of approval, the lead act made his entrance. Every sentence Commissioner Gordon uttered was punctuated by applause. He ended by growling, 'The fight goes on,' which prompted a standing ovation. Someone even shouted, 'More.'

'He's not going to say it all over again, is he?' said Matt. But even he was on his feet cheering.

Everyone seemed to be stirred, except Tara. They were acting as if everything was going to be all right; this night was turning into a celebration. But surely the most important fact about tonight was that none of the councillors who'd been invited had turned up. And they were the only ones with the power.

There were few worse things than being totally powerless; unable to stop your school closing or your boyfriend walking out on you. Now, what had made her think about Phil? The truth was she'd been thinking about him all day. She was having a bit of a relapse. That was all right. She'd been warned about the relapse. And she knew it wasn't really him she was mourning. It was the idea of him.

But suddenly tears were blurring her eyes. This was awful. How could she be so pathetic? She didn't want anyone to see her like this. She got to her feet. 'I won't be a minute,' she whispered to Katie. Then she edged her way out. Hardly anyone noticed her. They were too intent on cheering a parent-governor who was outlining the battle plan.

Battle plan! Don't they know the war's over? We lost.

Tara fled down the corridor intending to disappear into the ladies' but then she heard, 'Rayner is my school and it's not going to close.' The three generations were being filmed for posterity. Tara didn't want to walk into all that – now here's a girl who's so upset about her school closing she's started blubbing – so she fled out of a classroom door instead.

She'd intended to go home, lock herself in her room, and cry into her pillow, she was well practiced in doing that by now. Yet she also felt impatient with herself. Surely she was over him now? He was worthless, for goodness sake. She was well rid of him. She should be cheering.

Instead, she just felt defeated. Totally defeated.

She should go back, talk to Katie and Matt. They'd understand. They'd been such good friends to her. But enough was enough. It wasn't fair to bother them again. And besides, she didn't know exactly what she was feeling so depressed about. This was just a sort of free-floating misery that she'd suddenly caught, the way she might have caught a cold. If only she knew what the cure was.

Tara walked faster and faster. Where was she going? She hadn't a clue. Ahead of her loomed Hart Lane – she could cut through here next year when she went to Priestley High. But she didn't want to go there. That wasn't her school. Why did everything have to be so horrible and mixed up?

She started to walk down Hart Lane. The path was very narrow, few people used it now, and the overhanging branches made it seem as if you were setting off down a tunnel. Suddenly, in a burst of frustration, Tara kicked a stone high into the air, a spray of mud accompanying its journey. She raised her foot again. Anything was better than crying. Which stone should she send hurtling now? But then she let out a low gasp. She spotted the yellow beak first. The rest was partly camouflaged by the dim, grey light. She bent down and gazed at the blackbird lying very still. She wondered how it had died. It didn't seem to have been attacked. She stared a little closer, then gave a shudder: ants were scuttling over the body. Tara scooped up a pile of old leaves, they felt slushy and wet, then very gently she placed them over the blackbird. She wasn't sure why, but she felt she should say something, 'God bless you,' she whispered, 'sleep well.'

Feeling a little foolish, she got up. The clouds looked low and threatening. There was going to be an almighty downpour any moment. She should run home now. But first she took one peek through the branches at the field which stretched ahead of her; once horses had been there, a lovely brown horse she especially remembered. She'd had her picture taken with that horse, then she'd sent a copy to a penfriend and pretended the horse belonged to her. The penfriend believed her, and kept writing about how lucky Tara was . . . in the end Tara almost believed it too.

She smiled faintly at the memory. But the field was empty now, empty and bleak and . . .

Lightning filled the sky. At least that's what she thought it was. Only there wasn't just a flash of light, the light kept on growing. Until it was everywhere around her.

For a moment the shock of it seemed to freeze her brain. She just stood there, transfixed. But what was it? She started looking away from it, then looking back again thinking it would somehow disappear. If anything, it grew even brighter. She'd never seen such an intense light, but it wasn't burning her eyes at all. So where was it coming from? It must be the sun. But there wouldn't be any sun in the sky now.

So what was it?

She gazed around her. Everything looked so bright and warm. Only the warmth was inside her too, inside her head and in her bones. It was as if her whole body had been numb before and now new blood was starting to flow again, bringing her to life.

It was the most wonderful feeling. Somehow, she'd made a connection with something new that was showing her what life could be like. The light seemed to be reaching out to her.

It faded as suddenly as it had appeared and everything went back to greyness again.

Tara stared and stared into that field. But there was nothing now. Finally she stumbled away, almost bumping into a couple who were walking their two West Highland dogs. She watched the dogs sniffing around the nettles; it all seemed so normal and everyday, yet, just a few moments ago . . . She turned to the couple, both in their comfortable sweaters and old trousers.

'A few minutes ago, did you see something? This light, it was everywhere. You must have seen it.'

'Lightning, you mean,' pronounced the man.

'No, no,' gasped Tara, 'that's a harsh light and this was . . . beautiful.'

As soon as she said it she knew 'beautiful' was the wrong word.

She wasn't surprised they stepped back a couple of paces. And yet, the light had been beautiful.

'Well, it's certainly building up for rain,' said the woman after an awful pause. 'I expect we'll see lightning sometime tonight.' Her husband bobbed his head in agreement.

'Yeah, right, thanks,' said Tara hastily. 'Goodnight.'

She walked quickly away from them. They hadn't seen what she saw. And she knew neither had anyone else.

Only she had seen that light tonight.

That beautiful light.

Only she.

But why? What did it mean?

6 What has Tara seen?

'Come on then, Tara,' said Katie. 'I want to know everything.' They were both sitting in Katie's bedroom which was, as Katie described it, about the size of a downstairs loo. There was something very cosy about it all the same; added to which Katie's mum had a habit of leaving boxes of chocolate mints on Katie's dressing-table. The latest box lay between Katie and Tara as they sat cross-legged on the carpet.

'Something's put a smile on your face today,' Katie went on. 'Or someone?' she looked at Tara expectantly.

It was true, Tara couldn't help breaking out into smiles. She just felt so elated. Suddenly there was all this happiness bubbling up inside her. But wonderful as last night had been, she couldn't fit it into her life. It was too huge. What was she supposed to do with it? She needed someone to help her. There was only one candidate. Yet, even with Katie she felt nervous.

'Actually, I wrote down what happened last night in my diary,' said Tara. Feeling distinctly self-conscious, she produced her pale blue diary.

'I thought you'd thrown that away after . . .' began Katie.

'Yeah, well I tore out the pages for May, June and the first week of July, then I bunged it in the back of my wardrobe. But last night I found it again and started writing . . .'

'Wow,' exclaimed Katie. 'Hey, it's nothing to do with Paul, is it?'

'No, no,' said Tara, somewhat impatiently.

Downstairs the doorbell rang.

'Oh I hope that's not for me,' said Katie. 'I'm just going to die of curiosity here.'

Footsteps thumped up the stairs, and Matt opened the door and immediately crashed out on the carpet, his feet touching the door, his eyes closed. Katie giggled. 'Are you all right?'

'No, I'm dead,' muttered Matt.

'And aren't you supposed to be on a date?' said Tara.

'That's right, with that girl you saw at the ice-rink,' Katie added. 'Annette, wasn't it?'

'I've forgotten her name already,' said Matt.

'Why, what's happened?'

He gave a sigh which turned into a yawn. 'It takes energy chatting up girls, that's why I only do it once every two years, also . . .' the two girls leaned forward, '. . . also, she gave me a bell tonight to let me know that she's just started seeing someone else.'

'Oh, she's really messing you about, isn't she?' said Katie.

'Well, it's her loss,' said Tara.

'She's got fat legs anyway,' added Katie.

Matt sat up. 'That's true.' He grabbed four chocolate mints from the box.

'Hey, easy on those,' cried Katie.

'Oh come on, he is nursing a broken heart, aren't you?' said Tara.

Matt nodded, grinning and munching as he did so. Tara suspected Matt was quite upset about Annette. Not that he'd ever admit it. Of course, mingled with her sympathy for him was a certain amount of relief. She and Katie didn't really approve. She wasn't worthy of him.

'I'm glad you came back to us,' said Tara. Matt's only reply was to stuff two more chocolate mints into his mouth.

'And you picked a good moment. Tara's about to tell us about something wonderful that happened to her last night.'

'Am I old enough to hear this?' replied Matt. Almost without realising it, Tara had put her diary away. Much as she liked Matt, she didn't want to share last night's experience with him. Not yet anyway. This was for Katie's ears only.

'No, it's all right,' said Tara. 'It can wait.'

'But I can't,' exclaimed Katie.

'Secrets, secrets. Yes, I see,' said Matt. He got up. 'Cheerio chaps, I may be gone a while. Remember me sometimes, won't you?'

'Oh sit down, Captain Oates,' cried Tara. She didn't want Matt going off all insulted; he'd been messed about enough tonight. Matt thumped down again and stared at her. He was grinning faintly but there was a tension too; he was determined not to be left out of this.

'Well, look,' began Tara. 'I will tell you, but just remember, this is really important to me, all right?' That had come out far more aggressively than she'd intended. There was a wariness in Matt's face now – and in Katie's. They were wondering if she'd seen Phil, weren't they? She couldn't blame them. She used to talk about him in that same, defensive way.

She tried to shift gears. 'It's something so amazing I can't believe it.' They were still gazing warily at her. 'I left the meeting at the school early last night and I went for a walk. I ended up in Hart Lane,' she picked up her diary and read aloud. 'I saw this dead blackbird lying there and I covered him up with some leaves.'

'Aaah,' murmured Katie.

'Then I was looking out over the fields,' she looked up. 'You know where the horses used to be?' Katie nodded. 'And then I saw it.' Her voice cracked slightly as she read aloud. 'This great beam of light appeared from nowhere – a kind of golden light which made everything bright and warm; and that light . . . that light seemed alive. I felt it was showing me something.' She stopped. She was certain she was blushing. She felt sick with embarrassment. She should have kept last night hidden inside her.

'Well, say something,' said Tara. Matt and Katie were just staring at her.

'I wasn't expecting that,' murmured Katie.

'Neither was I,' replied Tara.

Matt leant across and started examining her arms.

'What are you doing?' Tara asked.

'Seeing if there are any strange marks on your arms,' said Matt. 'Then we'll know if you've been abducted or not.'

'Oh, ha ha,' snapped Tara.

'This is a wind-up, isn't it?' he said softly.

'No,' replied Tara firmly. 'It is not a wind-up.'

'So you were in Hart Lane and you saw this really bright light?' said Katie, her tone was placatory. 'Well, it does happen. I mean, there's a guy who works in Sainsbury's, he's always going on about this light he saw. I mean it happened years ago now, but he's still really serious about it. He's convinced he saw a UFO.'

'It wasn't a UFO,' said Tara.

'How do you know?' asked Matt.

Tara shook her head. 'I just do . . .'

'And you hadn't been anywhere near a pub?' asked Matt.

'Look, just forget I ever said anything,' snapped Tara.

'Oh, don't be like that,' said Katie. 'It's just . . .'

'A bit of a dodgy situation,' interrupted Matt.

'I don't think so,' said Tara.

'Well, not dodgy exactly...' he began. Both he and Katie were wearing an expression Tara knew well, a look that said, we're being patient and understanding with a friend who isn't herself. All summer she'd seen that look and been grateful for it. But tonight she was telling them about something really good. Why couldn't they see that?

'Look,' cried Katie. 'Why don't we go to Hart Lane now, have a look around there . . . the more facts we can find out the better.'

Tara was doubtful, but for once she found the enforced intimacy of Katie's room oppressive. 'Whatever you like,' she muttered.

Conversation on the way to Hart Lane was pretty ragged; even Matt was subdued. Over and over in her head Tara was wishing she hadn't said anything. The wind was in the trees tonight and the leaves shone with recent rain.

Tara pointed through the branches at the field. 'That's where I saw it, right there.' Her heart started to pound. This place would always be haunted for her. But when she saw their blank faces she felt awkward and rather foolish. 'I feel as if I'm on *Crimewatch* or something, returning to the scene of the crime.' Matt and Katie laughed nervously.

'Well, there's no bright light here tonight,' said Matt.

'Give it a chance,' said Katie.

'I don't think it works like that,' said Tara.

They stood there for a few more minutes then Matt said, 'Don't get mad, but maybe for a few minutes you just fell asleep.'

'No.' Tara struggled not to sound impatient.

'Or maybe you had a migraine,' suggested Katie. 'You do get them occasionally.'

'No, it was nothing like that. It was real.'

'Yet no one else saw it,' said Matt.

'I don't think so,' said Tara, remembering the old couple.

'But if you'd had a camera last night you could have photographed what you saw?' suggested Matt.

'Yes, I think so. I'm not sure.'

'I've got it,' cried Matt. 'I know what you saw last night: a tractor.'

'A tractor?' echoed Tara.

'Yeah, they're often out late at night and their lights can be very bright,' said Matt.

'Of course,' cried Katie, 'why didn't I think of that?' They were both grinning with relief.

'It wasn't a tractor,' said Tara shortly. 'This light I saw was immense, and anyway, the light from a tractor wouldn't make me feel . . . that light was personal and so full of love. It was beautiful.' She turned away from them.

'Well, people do see mysterious lights,' said Katie softly.

'And now Tara's seen the light,' said Matt, not unkindly.

She faced him. He grinned at her. And she smiled back. She felt he was saying, if you want to say you've seen a light that's all right with me, you're still my friend. But sometime later he and Katie would whisper about this together: Poor old Tara, she's had lots of stress lately, but if it helps her over her problems to think she saw a light, then where's the harm? Still, we must keep an eye on her all the same.

On the way back to Katie's Tara deliberately changed the subject. She was bright and chatty, but inside she couldn't help feeling they had both let her down.

The following night she didn't go round to Katie's. Her excuse was genuine: she had to finish an essay for history. But she also didn't fancy another evening with Katie and Matt asking her if she'd seen her light again, their eyes wide with scepticism and concern.

Meanwhile it was Nan and Grandad's fortieth wedding anniversary. Tara hated the way neighbours kept going on about this, it made her grandparents seem so old. The sitting-room table was now crammed with presents, including a box of chocolates from Tara, a bunch of flowers from her dad, and a huge red azalea in a basket from Paul. In the evening Nan and Grandad were going out for a meal. They hardly ever ate out, in fact, they hardly ever went out, not together anyway.

Tara watched Nan come down the stairs. She looked as uncertain as someone on her first date.

'How do I look, Tara?' Before she could answer, Nan rushed on, 'Like something the cat's dragged in, I know.' She gave a dry, humourless little laugh.

'Oh, Nan, you look lovely,' said Tara. Nan was wearing her pale blue suit with a white frilly blouse, she'd also put on pearl earrings and a pearl necklace which Tara hadn't seen her wear for years.

'You should dress up more often.'

'Not much point at my age,' said Nan. 'Still, I like to think I can still look smart.' She stared at her watch. 'Your grandfather said he'd just drop some model engines off at Ralph Smart's and he'd come right back. That was an hour ago.'

Paul appeared in the hallway. He gave a little whistle. 'Hey, don't you look nice.'

Nan's face lit up. 'Well you've got to make an effort now and again.' She stared at her watch. 'I don't know what he's playing at. We booked a table for eight o'clock and it's one minute to eight now.'

'They'll hold the table for you,' said Paul.

'Really? They don't like it if you're late though, do they? And I don't blame them . . . then he's got to get changed.'

'Why don't you ring Ralph Smart, see if Grandad's left yet?' asked Tara.

'I'd never hear the end of it,' replied Nan. 'It's typical of him: drives over there to deliver some model engine or other – that's no bother at all – but if it's anything for me . . . that's different. He never puts himself out for me. Oh well, it's too late now,' Nan's voice rose . . . 'Paul, will you ring and cancel for me please?'

'Oh no, Paul don't,' cried Tara.

'Shall we give him a few more minutes?' asked Paul reasonably.

'He'll be hours yet, thinks more of his friends than he does of me.' A key turned in the lock. Grandad started with surprise at the reception committee.

'You're late,' said Nan.

He glared at her. 'Plenty of time.'

'The table was booked for eight, it's gone eight now,' she murmured.

'We'd better go now then, hadn't we,' said Grandad, in that clipped tone he reserved for Nan.

'What, dressed like that?' she cried.

'My clothes are perfectly adequate,' said Grandad.

'You could at least have put your suit on,' said Nan. 'Surely that's not too much to ask. But it's all right, we won't go. Ring up and cancel, Paul. I'd rather not go now.' Grandad didn't answer he just thumped up the stairs.

Tara looked at Paul; she'd have been embarrassed at anyone else witnessing that little scene, but not Paul. She felt he was an insider too. They exchanged quick smiles while Nan ranted on. Grandad came downstairs in his suit. He winked at Tara as if to say, isn't this a load of nonsense, and said to Nan, 'Ready for the off, then?'

'I've been ready for the best part of an hour.'

'Shall I ring up and say you'll be a little late?' asked Paul.

'Would you, Paul, dear, it's Lautrec's restaurant – number's on the pad – and would you apologise for our lateness.' Grandad was already outside. Nan half-ran after him, turning round at the door to declare, 'I'd just as soon not go if it's going to be like this. Why can't we ever go out nicely?'

Tara and Paul waved them off together. Tara felt almost as if she and Paul were parents seeing off two of their quarrelsome offspring. 'They're wild, your grandparents, aren't they?' said Paul.

From anyone else Tara wouldn't have been sure how to take that, but with Paul she just grinned and said, 'They never stop amazing me. Nan loved the azalea, by the way, they're her favourites. I like them too, although pink roses are my favourite.' Then, in case that sounded too much like a hint, she added quickly, 'Well, pink roses were my mum's favourite, she had them in her wedding bouquet, so I suppose that's why I like them too.'

Paul nodded as if he was interested, then said, 'Well, I'd better go and ring up Lautrec's.'

This was Tara's cue to disappear into the sitting-room, that's what she should do; she had English and History essays to write. Instead she found herself saying to Paul, 'Would you like a cup of tea?'

'That would be great.'

Tara half-skipped into the kitchen. This didn't mean he wanted to talk to her. He was probably only being polite; or maybe he was just thirsty. She felt quite giddy with pleasure.

Suddenly he was standing beside her in the kitchen. She twittered on about Nan and Grandad's antics, then to her surprise he suddenly changed the subject: 'I was going to ask you if everything was all right.'

'With me? Oh, everything's fine. Why?'

He gave a shy grin. 'I don't know, it's just last night at dinner you seemed far away . . . troubled. And at breakfast, too.' She was amazed – and touched – that he'd even noticed. 'I wondered if you were worried about the school closing.'

'Yes, I was,' began Tara.

'Well, we're going to make a fight of it. This school is part of the village. If it goes, then something vital in the village dies too. That's why we're sending a massive petition to County Hall next week and I'm meeting a friend in local television who's got some publicity ideas so . . . don't worry, Tara, all right?' He said this so kindly Tara didn't quite know how to reply. But it didn't matter. He was already walking into his room. 'Cheers for the tea. My turn to make some later.'

She should go through his room to the sitting-room, get on with those essays. Instead she hovered awkwardly by the dining-room table.

He was now sitting in his chair, looking through a pile of exercise books, his left leg tapping away as he did so. He never seemed able to sit still, one or other foot was always moving, as if in time to music only he could hear.

He looked up at Tara. He must be wondering why she was still here. Why was she? She just knew there seemed a strange inevitability about what she said next, as if somewhere it had already been spoken.

'Actually, there was something else,' she smiled nervously. 'Have you got a minute?'

'Sure,' he waved her into the chair opposite him.

'This is going to sound really strange.'

He grinned good-humouredly.

She started telling him what she'd seen on Monday night. Even without her diary she felt she described it better this time, perhaps because she felt less self-conscious.

Paul didn't interrupt her. He sat there absorbed and when she'd finished he seemed stunned by what she'd told him.

'This is truly amazing,' he said finally.

'So what should I do?'

'Treasure it,' he said gently.

She repeated those words to herself. She liked the way he had said that. 'But what was it?'

He squinted his eyes for a moment as if thinking really hard. 'It's a gift – a gift for you.' Then he added, almost apologetically, 'Of course, I'm one of those people who brings God into everything, so I would say it's a gift from God.' He stopped. 'Do you want me to say any more?'

Tara nodded. To her surprise she did.

'You see, God is trying to get through to us all the time. He loves us so he wants us to know him. But mostly we shut God out. Yet he never stops trying to reach us . . .'

'That's what I felt,' interrupted Tara. 'As if the light was reaching out for me in some way. I did say a prayer – a very brief one – just before . . .' she hesitated.

'For a moment your defences were down,' said Paul. 'So God could come through and show you how life could be, for eternity.'

Tara felt herself pulling away from him now. This was all too much, too fast. As if sensing this, Paul said, 'Sorry. I get carried away.'

'No . . . it was interesting.'

'God's salesman, that's what some people call me,' he gave an ironic smile. 'It's just . . . well if you see a really brilliant film, you want to tell everyone about it, don't you. So when you've found this absolutely brilliant message which will save people's lives . . .' he gave another rather sad smile.

She wasn't sure what to say. 'How did your Christian Union meeting go yesterday?'

'A few of my form loyally turned up, but no one else, a little bit disappointing really, still . . . early days.'

Tara couldn't help feeling sorry for him. 'I think some people find it hard to commit.'

'That's it,' cried Paul. 'And I can understand that. Even after I saw the cross and I knew there was something in it, I still didn't do anything, not for weeks. Until I saw this special service advertised in the paper, so I went along. It was in a hall and I hovered about outside for ages.' He grinned at the memory. 'Finally I was brave and went in, and I couldn't believe it. The few times I'd been to church with Alan and Joyce, my foster-parents, had been dull and boring, but here I walked in and there was a lot of music, people were singing their hearts out and everyone was just so happy and friendly.

'Then this young guy came up to me and chatted. He introduced me to his mates and said, "We're going away next weekend, would you like to come along?" He started telling me where they were going, it sounded great, but I told them I didn't have any money. Do you know what they said? "Don't worry, we'll pay." ' He shook his head. 'Normally that would have sent all sorts of alarm bells ringing, but they were just so genuine. It knocked me out. I've never felt so welcome anywhere as I did that night. I knew it wasn't just the people, it was God. When I left there, I tell you, I was just grinning like a Cheshire cat.'

Tara gazed at him, thinking his eyes were amazing when they looked full at you: wide, strikingly brown, hypnotic.

'And you've been a Christian ever since?'

He considered this. 'Yes. Although my faith's been tested, especially when I wanted to be an actor.'

'Why, what happened then?'

'Well, before I found God I loved acting more than anything else in the world. When I became a Christian I carried on acting and, with the help of Alan and Joyce, I even got into an acting school.'

'I didn't know that,' exclaimed Tara.

'Oh yeah, I did,' he said proudly, 'and if I say it myself, I was OK, even got a part in a play in London. They were really tough auditions so I was very pleased. But then I read the play and it was full of things against Christ so I rang up the director and he said, "Oh, come on," ' Paul started to give a devastating impression of a plummy, luvvie voice. ' "Christianity's an outmoded concept in the twentieth century, and if you turn this play down you'll have to give back your Equity card and you'll never work again." '

'And is that what happened?'

'Pretty much,' said Paul. 'Never regretted my decision, though.'

Tara stared at him incredulously. 'Not ever?'

'Take my faith out of me and you lose the man,' said Paul, simply.

To give up your greatest ambition, your chance of fame and fortune just because of a belief . . . Tara could never do that. But she was intrigued all the same. In fact, she was leaning so far forward their knees were almost touching. They carried on talking until Tara heard her grandparents' car. She jumped to her feet as if she'd been caught doing something she shouldn't.

'Well, I'd better go and do my essays.' She looked at the clock, 'It's nearly half past ten. I'm sorry.'

He was on his feet too. 'No, I really enjoyed your company.' Tara hoped she wasn't blushing. 'And what you told me. It's so exciting.'

'Yes,' she gasped. Car doors were banging now. 'Well, bye.'

'Tara,' he called after her. 'Will you do me a favour?'

'Yes, sure.'

'If you get a moment tonight will you just read the first couple of chapters of John's Gospel?'

She smiled at him. 'Yes, all right.'

'I just thought it might help form a bridge to what you've seen.'

Tara doubted this but she was curious to see what he'd picked for her to read. She said, 'Only thing is, it's a bit embarrassing actually, I know we've got a Bible somewhere, but . . .'

Paul jumped in, 'Here, have mine.'

'Oh no, I couldn't.'

'It's all right, I've got another one upstairs.'

'Only one?' she teased.

He grinned good-naturedly, 'This is the one I was given at school.' She took it from him. It was a small pocket New Testament with a green cover.

There was barely time even to say thank you. She dived into the sitting-room just as Nan turned the key in the lock. Tara was sitting on the sofa with a book on her lap when Nan and Grandad looked in.

'Not still working, are you?' said Grandad.

'It has to be done,' sighed Tara. 'Anyway, how was the meal?'

Grandad raised his eyes to the heavens.

'Well,' said Nan, 'no one cooks vegetables how I like them, they're always too hard. And they put far too much salt in the soup. I'm sure that's to make you buy more drinks . . .'

'But you enjoyed it?' asked Tara.

'Oh, very much,' said Nan. 'It's just nice to get out. I'm worried about you working so hard, though.'

Would Nan stop worrying if she knew Tara had spent the whole time talking to Paul?

Later, she lay in bed looking through the New Testament. She felt rather self-conscious at first. She turned to the front of the Bible. There was a label on which was printed: THE NEW TESTAMENT AND PSALMS. PRESENTED BY THE GIDEONS TO . . . and there was Paul's surprisingly shaky signature. She wondered how old he was when he signed that. Maybe he was her age, fourteen. She tried to picture him then, casually signing his name, quite unaware how this book was going to play such an important role in his life.

And how he'd given the book to her. That seemed significant too, somehow.

She started reading the first two chapters of John, headed, 'The coming of Christ'. If Kate and Matt knew she was doing this, they'd burst out laughing. 'What's he doing, setting you homework now?' they'd say.

The first few lines read rather like poetry. They had a strange rhythm to them. And then she saw why Paul had selected these passages: line after line referred to Jesus as 'the light – the real light which enlightens every man.'

Tara gave a shiver. That light she'd seen, could it in some way have come from God? There had been moments when she had considered this. Once she had even tried praying – something she hadn't done seriously for years. But she'd immediately felt awkward and self-conscious, and stopped. Tonight, though, she whispered, 'Was the vision from you, God? If it was, thank you, but I need more proof.' Then she drifted off to sleep.

Tara woke with a jump. Someone was banging on her door.

'Yes,' she cried.

But the sound was coming from downstairs. Someone was hammering on the door. She held her watch up to her face. It was half past twelve.

She heard Grandad mutter something, then trudge downstairs.

Tara stumbled to the landing. Nan was already there. 'We never get callers at this time,' she declared. 'I hope your father's all right.' Despite herself Tara couldn't help feeling anxious too.

Downstairs, bolts were slowly, carefully, being pulled back.

'Yes, what is it?' croaked her grandad.

Tara couldn't hear the reply, just Grandad exclaiming, 'What, now? This is outrageous.'

7 Late-night caller

Grandad switched on the hall light. 'Well, you'd better come in.' Then, wheezing slightly, he came back up to the landing, where Nan and Tara were hovering.

'Who is it?' hissed Nan at once.

'It's a girl demanding to see Paul now, calls herself Clare.'

'Oh, what a relief,' declared Nan. Then she went on, 'I know who Clare is, she rang Paul the first day he was here, remember?'

'No,' grunted Grandad, 'I don't.'

But Tara remembered. She also remembered how Paul hadn't exactly rushed to ring her back.

'I wonder what she wants at this time of night,' said Nan.

In reply, Grandad went and banged on Paul's door. 'You've got a visitor – Clare.'

A couple of minutes later Paul sprang out of his bedroom. He was just wearing a brightly coloured dressing-gown, nothing else. He looked really shaken: 'She's down there now?' He raced down the dark stairs.

'Do you think I should ask them if they want a cup of tea?' asked Nan.

'I should think all they want is some privacy,' replied Grandad, propelling Nan back into their bedroom. He turned to Tara, 'Try and get back to sleep as soon as you can, love . . . the excitement's over for tonight.'

Tara nodded solemnly. As soon as her grandparents were tucked safely away, she sneaked back out on to the landing and down the stairs, telling herself she wasn't being nosy. Paul had helped her tonight, now maybe she could help him.

But she still couldn't hear properly. She stepped on to the next step which creaked ominously. She froze. Then Clare cried out, 'But is that all, is that the only problem?'

Tara couldn't catch Paul's reply – he was speaking very softly – then Clare exclaimed, 'You know I don't mean that. I'm just saying, if that's all that's standing between us . . .' then her voice rose so shrilly Tara was certain even her grandparents would hear. 'But what about us? Don't we count for anything?'

Paul's voice remained frustratingly low. Tara strained forward.

Then all at once they were both in the hallway. Tara darted behind the banisters but not before she'd glimpsed Clare: honey-blonde hair, dazzlingly white silk blouse, dismayingly pretty. 'Don't worry, I shan't bother you again,' Clare almost shrieked. She sounded hysterical. 'Don't worry about me.'

Paul followed her outside. 'Look, don't go like this,' he called. Tara never heard what Clare said. She slipped back into her bedroom just as Paul ran upstairs again.

Over breakfast Paul apologised for his late-night visitor, and in the evening he apologised all over again. Otherwise, he hardly said anything. He was polite but distant. He had not changed out of his grey suit. Nan had noticed this too, but when she suggested having a word Grandad replied sharply, 'The last thing he wants is us interfering.' He said 'us' but actually he meant Nan.

Nan shook her shoulders like a sulky schoolgirl. 'Neighbours are always knocking on my door wanting advice. Of course your grandad never sees any of that stuck up in his loft.' But Nan didn't say anything to Paul.

Tara decided it was up to her.

She sat in her room listening to a Blur tape. Since she'd found out Paul liked them they'd become one of her favourite bands too. She rehearsed what she'd say. She'd be very casual and tentative at first, so if he didn't want to talk she could quickly flee.

She crept stealthily down the stairs. Feeling both nervous and excited, she opened the door. The room was in total darkness. She blundered forward. He started in his chair.

'I just . . .' she stopped. What was she supposed to say? 'Can I talk to you for a minute, please?' No, that wasn't right. But already he was replying.

'Sure, of course.'

She stumbled into the chair opposite him. His brown eyes were lit by the light of the fire. 'Shall I put on a light?' he asked.

'Oh no, that's all right.' She preferred the room like this with all the odd, distracting clutter blotted out. Now it seemed touched with mystery.

'It's just, sometimes it's easier to think in the dark,' he said.

'I find that too.'

She sensed him looking at her enquiringly. The darkness made her bold. 'I just wondered how you were, you didn't seem quite yourself tonight.' She paused.

'Was it that obvious? Oh my gosh.' Tara had noticed how Paul sometimes used old-fashioned phrases which, like his beautiful manners, seemed to belong to another age. She rather liked it. 'Anyhow, you're right. I'm not too pleased with myself, T-a-r-a.' He stretched her name out as if he were savouring it. 'Did you hear what happened last night?'

'A bit,' replied Tara, not sure what she was supposed to know.

'Clare, the girl who was here last night, was my girlfriend for nearly six months. She is a very nice girl, beautiful, funny, warm-hearted . . . I care about her a lot. But we had to break up. There was no other way because I was in such agony . . .' he rubbed his hands over his face.

Then, speaking more slowly than before, 'Clare is not a Christian, she doesn't even know if she believes in God. She did come to a service once and said she had quite enjoyed it.' He shook his head bemusedly, 'So I said to her, "Did you go to that service because you wanted to know God, or to please me?" But she didn't need to tell me the answer. She was humouring me. It meant nothing to her at all, you know. And the whole situation was just tearing me apart, it was like . . . it was like your girlfriend never getting on with your best friend, never wanting to talk about him, never wanting to know him, never wanting to be with him . . . Clare was cutting me off from God. That's why I ended it. I had no choice . . .' His words jammed together. 'I tried to explain it to her, make her see it was the best thing for both of us. I thought she understood. But then she kept ringing me, telling me we loved each other and that was all that mattered, but it isn't.

'And then last night there she was saying the same things . . . and I felt so . . . When I was about seven I had mumps very badly. The pain was so strong it made me cry out, and Joyce used to say to me: "Is the bad man making you dance again?" And I'd say, "Yeah, Aunty Joyce, the bad man's making me dance . . ." and now it's like I'm the bad man who's making Clare dance . . . can't deal with it,' he added suddenly, desperately.

Tara had been listening to him with a kind of wonderment. It was as if she were talking to him in a dream, in which they dropped all their masks and spoke from the heart. She heard herself saying, 'A couple of months ago I was dumped, you know. Only the boy in question never actually told me himself, so I pestered him with phone calls, even a silly letter. He ignored them all. But if he had bothered to talk to me, I'm not saying it wouldn't still have been painful – it would – but at least he would have shown me I still existed and that would have helped me . . . let him go.' She trembled as she talked. 'Now Clare's got to let you go, you've talked it through with her, done everything you can, you've acted like a gentleman.'

'A gentleman,' he repeated the words with amusement and yet, a kind of pride, too. Then there was silence again, but it was a good silence.

'That helped me,' he said finally. 'Thank you, Tara.'

'Well, you helped me last night so . . . by the way, I've read the first two chapters of John like you suggested, and then I carried on, I didn't want to stop.' She was showing off now, letting him see that unlike Clare, she was genuinely interested.

'Hey, that's great,' he yelled so enthusiastically Tara couldn't help smiling.

'Look, Tara, I don't know if you're at all interested, but there's going to be an open meeting at Finley Community Centre next Saturday night. It's for Christians and non-Christians and it's very friendly and informal, a chance for everyone to get together and ask some questions and have fun.' Aware he'd come on too strong he added: 'But don't feel you have to say anything now. I don't want to put you on the spot, so . . .'

'I'd love to go, honestly,' interrupted Tara.

'But that's brilliant. Finley's about fifteen kilometres away but I could always drive us. I'm not sure exactly where it is so you could be my plucky navigator. Tell you what, I've got some tickets on me somewhere.' He dug into his pockets. 'Yeah, here we go,' he handed her a small green ticket. 'Don't worry if you lose it.'

'I won't lose it,' she cried fervently.

Their hands touched just as the room was flooded in glaring, orange light.

'Tara, are you . . . yes, there you are. What are you doing sitting in the dark?'

Tara blinked at Nan in bewilderment. What was Nan doing here breaking in upon Tara's beautiful dream with such mundane questions? And Matt, where had he come from? He was standing in the doorway, too.

Tara glanced down at her ticket then closed her hand up tightly.

'Didn't you hear me calling you, Tara?' Nan went on.

'No,' said Tara shortly. She was very fond of her nan, but at this moment if she could have vaporised her out of existence she'd have done it.

Nan turned to Paul. 'I hope Tara's not getting you to do her homework.'

Tara had to smile. Did Nan really think they'd been sitting in the dark doing homework? Or was Nan just saying that to cover up her embarrassment? And what was Matt thinking about it all? Why couldn't Nan and Matt just slip away, switching off the lights as they went?

'Tara and I were just talking about things,' said Paul.

'I see,' said Nan in a tone which indicated she didn't at all. 'Well, I'll leave you then . . . I'm sure Matt would appreciate a cup of tea and a biscuit.' She departed somewhat huffily.

Matt lowered his cap. 'Evening all . . . not interrupting anything, am I?' There was a mocking edge to his tone which Tara immediately resented.

'You two have met, haven't you?'

'I've seen you around the school,' said Matt, turning to Paul. 'Bit weird seeing you in the evening in Tara's house, not even sure what to call you.'

'Hey, Paul, of course,' he replied, getting up and extending a hand to Matt. 'I'm pleased to meet you.'

'And so you should be. I'm Mr Armstrong – no, joke, I'm Matt as you may have heard.'

As they shook hands Tara got to her feet. She didn't want to stay here with Matt making his silly cracks, and his eyes brimming with curiosity. She walked to the door. 'See you later then, Paul.'

'See you Tara,' he replied, equally casually. The masks were back on now. The spell was broken.

She and Matt went upstairs to her room. 'Do you remember when I first came round and your nan made you keep your bedroom door open?'

'Oh, that was years and years ago,' she said impatiently.

'No, it wasn't. What are you talking about?' He was grinning at her, but he sounded indignant, even hurt.

In Tara's room Matt would usually fling himself on to her rocking-chair in the corner. But tonight, he prowled around her room as if he'd never been there before. He began examining the brushes and make-up bottles on her dressing-table with exaggerated interest. 'It all looked very cosy down there.'

'Paul was consulting me about something,' said Tara, unable to stop her voice swelling with pride.

'Ho, ho,' said Matt.

This was her cue to tell him what Paul had said. But she couldn't; it was too private. Matt would only spoil it.

He picked up one of her combs. He looked like a detective searching for clues. 'Agony aunt to the teachers, well, one teacher, anyway.'

'Will you stop walking around my room like that. You're making me dizzy.'

'Can't. I'm in training for this sponsored walk next week, trying to get a fighting fund to . . .' he assumed a hearty, upper-class voice, 'save the honour of the school, all that rot. Are you in?'

'Well, I'm already in the sponsored netball tournament, but yes, all right. How far have we got to walk?'

'Twenty kilometres.'

'You're going to walk twenty kilometres!' she exclaimed. 'Fifteen metres is your limit, isn't it?'

'True, but for the glory of Rayner School . . . did you know Glenn Jones is leaving this Friday?'

'No, when did you hear that?'

'Tonight. His parents say he may as well go to Priestley High now as next September. Nothing like a little faith, is there? Some more first years are bailing out too . . . soon there'll be only thee, me and Katie left. But we don't care, do we?'

'No, we'll go down with the school.'

He flashed her a smile. Tara felt some of her old affection for him returning.

'You know, Paul's arranged some good publicity. He's got his mate from the local television to come back . . .'

'I've heard. We've all got to sit around the school holding sweaty hands . . . I can't wait. So how are you?' he added, suddenly.

'I'm fine. Why?'

'I just wondered.' He picked up her old coffee mug, gazed at the decaying remains inside, made a face and asked, 'You haven't seen any more strange lights, then?'

'No, just the one, this month. And it wasn't so much strange as beautiful. You and Katie aren't keeping an eye on me, are you?'

He put the coffee mug down. 'You might say that.'

'Well, there's no need,' she was both touched and annoyed.

'We just don't want you . . .'

'Yes?'

He faced her. 'We just think you're a bit susceptible at the moment to . . . Were you two holding hands?'

'What?'

'When we came in, it looked like . . .'

'He was giving me a ticket.'

'What is he, a bus conductor in his spare time?'

She showed him the ticket. He started reading aloud in a moronic voice. 'The Good News. Come and chat informally with Christians about . . .'

Tara quickly slipped the ticket away again.

Matt smiled to himself.

'After new blood, is he?'

'No! That's a horrible thing to say.'

'Ah, but they like new blood, you know. I bet he's on the phone now.' He put on a Bela Lugosi accent: 'I think we've caught another one and she is going to be my masterpiece.'

Tara was smiling at Matt but she wasn't really amused. 'You don't know anything about Paul . . . just because he's a Christian.'

'I've nothing against Christians.'

'It sounds like it.'

Now Matt assumed the manner of a professor on a late-night discussion programme, 'No, we all need something to prop up our shaky lives.'

'Oh, very good.'

He bowed. 'But think about it, at school the people who've got no credibility are the ones who latch on to really extreme things. Overnight they become heavy metal freaks and wear really tight jeans, or they become Christians and join a clique of blokes in woolly jumpers and . . .'

'OK,' she interrupted, 'I get the idea. But what about you then? What are you into?'

'Oh, I'm a freelance, but then I have got an IQ of about six billion.'

'At least . . . so tell me this then, Professor Six Billion, what's the meaning of life?'

'The meaning of life, my child, is going to parties, having a good time and watching *The X Files* . . .' he dived on to her rocking-chair. 'You reproduce and then you snuff it.'

'And that's it?'

'That's all we're here to do, we're just sophisticated animals. The rest is hocus-pocus. But *you*'ve got credibility and amazingly brilliant friends who care about you, so you don't need to join the sad people in anoraks talking about the day their hamsters died and they found God. You've got it all here, already,' he gazed imploringly at her.

'I know I've got good friends,' said Tara warmly.

Matt looked as if he wanted to say something else but instead he stood up again. 'Will you do me a big, big favour, Tara?'

'Probably not. Go on then.'

'Don't go to this Save Your Souls meeting.'

Tara was startled both by the request and by the intense way Matt was staring at her.

'But why?'

'Because at the moment you're a bit vulnerable, and . . . you're not going to like this . . . but I think it could be dangerous.'

8 Paul in danger

Tara stared out of the car window. The rain beat against it, while a dark mysterious landscape rolled past.

She was off to the meeting at Finley. Matt should never have asked her not to go. All that nonsense about it being dangerous. Just because he'd closed his mind off didn't mean Tara had to. Still, he was quite gracious about it when she told him. He just gave this sad little smile and said, 'OK, if that's what you really want.' But he still made her feel as if she was letting him down.

She had invited him to join her but he only gave that sad little smile again and said, 'Reckon you need a chaperone, do you?' and then changed the subject. However, Katie was here, stretched out in the back. In fact, Katie's presence was vital. Tara's nan was being absurd about Paul: 'I don't understand why you two were sitting in the dark.'

'We just wanted to talk,' said Tara.

'You don't need the light off to talk,' replied Nan, firmly.

Tara sighed. Her nan could be so conventional sometimes.

'Now Tara, I don't want you bothering Paul.'

'What do you mean?'

'Well, that is his room and he's probably too polite to tell you to get out.'

'Nan, it isn't like that.'

'So what is it like?' Nan immediately fixed Tara with one of her stares.

Tara hesitated. She felt as if she'd fallen into a trap. How could she ever explain it to Nan? She couldn't. It was far too personal. In the end she took a deep breath and said: 'You know Paul's a Christian.'

'Yes.'

'Well, Katie's become very interested in Christianity, but Matt's dead against it, so I've been finding out things in secret for her from Paul.'

Nan visibly relaxed.

'And now there's a special meeting in Finley and Katie's desperate to go . . .'

'And so she should. You know, I was quite religious once.'

'You!'

'Oh yes. I didn't feel right if I didn't go to church on Sunday, went every week right up until I got married. Of course, your grandfather was never interested . . . So will you go with Katie?'

Tara played it cool. 'Not sure. I thought I might.'

Nan nodded approvingly.

Katie burst out laughing when Tara told her what she'd done, 'I never thought I'd spend a Saturday going off with a teacher in his car to a religious meeting.'

Tara had to smile as well. 'But you will come?'

'Well, I'm supposed to be seeing my dad then.' Katie's parents were separated and she spent alternate weekends with her father. 'But I'm sure I can fix that . . . mind you I'm not sure I should be encouraging this. I think you two are getting very serious.'

This was a kind of game she and Katie played. Katie acting as if Paul was a prospective boyfriend and interpreting everything he did as further proof of his romantic interest, while Tara denied the whole thing strenuously. And yet, in the back of her mind there was this voice calling softly . . . 'But anything's possible.'

The car stopped. 'Sorry I can't offer you door-to-door service,' said Paul, 'but apparently there's no parking at the community centre.'

'Typical,' declared Katie. She stepped outside. 'It's just chucking it down too.'

'Hey, look, you two have this,' Paul handed the girls his umbrella. 'I'll make a run for it.'

'But you'll get soaked,' cried Tara.

'Faster than a speeding bullet, that's me. It's just down the end of the road on the left. See you there.'

They watched him run off. 'Actually, he's not much slower than a speeding bullet,' observed Katie. 'And so gallant too . . . don't think much of where he's brought us, though.'

Tara could dimly remember visiting Finley years ago with her grandparents. It had been quite a thriving small town but most of the small shops had been wiped out by rising rents. It had a shabby, neglected air. Gangs of lads were hanging around the fast-food places. Wedged between a pub and a massive Everything-For-A-Pound shop was the small dilapidated Finley Community Centre.

Inside the hallway Paul was catching his breath. 'Not quite what I was expecting,' he said. There was no one there except for a man in a purple shell suit who was smoking a cigarette while gazing round furtively.

Paul went over to him. The man immediately tensed. 'Excuse me, we're looking for the main hall.'

'Right down the end there,' he snapped.

Paul reached the main hall first. He stood staring through the glass doors in confusion. Tara quickly saw why. The room was full of people only slightly older than herself, sitting in rows of desks, writing. They looked as if they were taking an exam. But surely not at this time of night?

Paul tentatively opened the door and immediately heard, 'All the fours, forty-four, two and six, twenty-six.'

'They're playing Bingo!' he exclaimed incredulously. 'Excuse me, my friends,' he called out.

'Sssh,' hissed at least ten people.

He quickly closed the door again. 'I know we're a bit early but . . . never fear I'll check out what's going on. Why don't you go and have a cup of coffee and whatever else they're serving up here – probably squashed flies or something – and I'll catch you up very shortly.' He wiped away some of the rain which was still dripping down his face. 'Going well, isn't it?' he said with a wry smile.

Inside the coffee shop red plastic chairs were stacked uninvitingly on top of the tables. 'We're closed,' declared a girl with ginger hair who was eating a packet of crisps.

'Is it OK if we just sit down for a minute?' asked Tara.

'I suppose so,' said the girl. 'Bingo finished then?' she asked in a rather more interested tone.

'No, not yet,' replied Tara.

'You're better off with the lottery, aren't you?' declared the girl. 'That's really big money.'

Without waiting for an answer she disappeared. Tara and Katie sat down. Katie started to sing: 'Saturday night at Finley Community Centre is where I like to be . . . Tell me Tara, what is it about this place you like so much?'

'I think it's all the wonderful white walls, they give the place such a warm atmosphere.'

'It's a shame Matt's not here. This is so tacky he'd have loved it.'

'I did invite him.'

'You know that Annette's been sniffing around him again, don't you?'

'Matt'd never consider her, not after the way she messed him around last time . . . Katie, if tonight is a total disaster you won't say anything to Paul, will you?'

'As if I would! And anyway, I'm enjoying it – in a warped kind of way.'

It was some minutes before Paul reappeared.

'So do we need to brush up on our Bingo?' called Katie.

'No, it's all been sorted out,' said Paul, rubbing his hands together excitedly. 'The Bingo has overrun but they were great about it when I explained. I did say that anyone who wanted to stay on for our meeting would be very welcome. After all they're looking to transform their lives too; they're just looking in the wrong place, that's all.'

Tara wanted to say, Oh, come on now, but when she looked at Paul, something stopped the words coming. Instead, she asked, 'So are there many people there?'

'It's building up nicely,' he replied.

Tara had the feeling Paul would say this even if there were only two men and a dog. But people were streaming inside now. A good-looking boy seated at a desk, wearing a white T-shirt with the words 'Something More' emblazoned on it, took their tickets and smiled hopefully at them. 'You're very welcome. I'm Mark, by the way. Feel free to ask me any questions later.'

'I've got a question for him already,' whispered Katie. 'What's his phone number?'

Inside the hall people milled around; most were the girls' age, although all ages were present. There were some families, too. Chairs were arranged in a semicircle, but the only occupant so far was a woman in the front row breast-feeding her baby.

Paul brought the girls two beakers of coffee. 'I found a coffee machine. You must be gasping for a drink.' Then he was greeted by someone he knew and was swept away.

Katie sipped the coffee appreciatively. 'That was really thoughtful of him.' She looked around her. 'They're not all sad people, are they? There are actually some quite decent-looking boys here.' Then she groaned. 'I don't believe it, there's Olivia Jackson.'

'What's she doing here?' demanded Tara at once.

Olivia Jackson was a girl from their year whom neither Tara nor Katie liked. She had a gushing, flirty manner and was renowned for stealing other girls' boyfriends.

'Oh Tara, Katie, hi,' she exclaimed. 'Great to see you.'

'We're really surprised to see you here,' replied Tara sharply.

'Well, Paul was going on about it – you know how he does – so I thought, why not? Actually, Mary,' she nodded at the girl who was standing beside her, 'and I, have a special reason for being here.'

Before she could say any more a girl in a Something More T-shirt came up, gave them a busy air-hostess smile and said, 'Excuse me, we're about to start so if you'd like to take your seats . . .'

'See you later then,' said Tara to Olivia. She didn't want to spend another second talking to her.

As soon as they were out of earshot Tara muttered, 'What was Paul doing inviting Olivia, of all people?'

'Now, don't be jealous.'

Tara laughed. But actually, she was very jealous – and hurt. She'd assumed Paul had only asked her; that's what had made tonight so special. Then she spotted two girls from Paul's Christian Union group. They were hovering in the doorway with their parents, and turned bright pink with pleasure when Paul went over to them.

As if reading her thoughts, Katie said, 'I expect Paul had to invite a few other people; Christians are pretty hot on getting new recruits, you know.'

'I know,' said Tara in a small voice. Then a diminutive greying figure in Ray-Bans asked Tara if the seat next to her was taken. She hesitated, then said, 'No, it isn't.' Why should she save a seat for Paul? Let him sit with Olivia Jackson.

'Is this your first time here?' the man asked.

'Yes it is.'

'It's my fourth. If you want any food afterwards you have to get in there fast. It goes really quickly.'

'Right, thanks,' said Tara.

Everyone was making their way to the remaining chairs. Tara noticed Paul scanning the rows for her and Katie. He sighted them, raised his thumb, then sat down somewhere at the back.

The noise died away as a young man in black Levis, black Kickers and a Something More T-shirt stood in front of them. He smiled politely until he had everyone's attention. 'I'm Jake,' he pointed to his name badge, 'which I hope you can see,' he laughed nervously, as if he'd made a joke. 'I just wanted to welcome you all, but especially all the new faces; it's really good to have you among us. Now, don't worry, you're not going to have to listen to me for very long.' Another nervous laugh. 'The purpose of tonight is for us to express briefly in words and music what our faith means to us, and then to give you a chance to chat informally and ask us anything – yes anything – you want.' He gave another laugh, which he turned into a cough.

'Do you think I could ask him how much his jeans cost?' whispered Katie.

'But first – some music.'

Four girls and one boy went through a medley of songs about Jesus being their saviour, accompanied by another boy on a guitar. The songs were surprisingly rousing. Little groups of people even stood up and started swaying and clapping.

'Oh no,' murmured Katie.

'They're all right,' replied Tara, defensively. 'They're just enjoying themselves.'

After they'd finished, a boy ran forward, carrying a large box. On it was written: ADDICTIONS. More people rushed up to him handing him other boxes on which were written things like: FAMILY. WORK. RELATIONSHIPS. MONEY. Soon the boy was tottering under the weight of them all.

'Any second now he's going to drop that lot,' whispered Katie.

Then a voice off-stage cried, 'Let me help you.' The boy shook his head. 'I'm here to help you,' called the voice. The boy shook his head again, breathing heavily from the pain of carrying all the boxes. 'Please let me help you,' beseeched the voice.

'No, go away, leave me alone, I don't need you,' said the boy, his face contorted in agony. Then, all at once he yelled, 'I can't cope! I can't cope!' and toppled forward, sending all the boxes flying.

The boy sank down on to his knees, 'I'm just so lost,' he gasped, then he buried his head in his hands. Tara knew exactly what he was feeling. She leaned forward just as a small middle-aged man with shoulder-length black hair and bright ruddy cheeks walked on to the stage. He was wearing a pale, short-sleeved shirt, check trousers and loafers.

'Hello, my name's John Morley.' There were murmurs around the hall which he acknowledged with a wry smile. 'Yes, you may have heard me on the radio on Sunday mornings, in what I believe they call the "God slot". People tell me I look better on the radio.' Another wry smile.

'That boy,' he said, pointing at the figure still crouched in the corner, 'was me.'

He went on to say how for the first eighteen years of his life he just lived for himself. 'And by the way, that's what sin is, when you always say, "Me first". Have you ever said that?' He smiled at the audience as if he already knew the answer. 'I know I have, many, many times. Oh yes, I did all the things we're supposed to enjoy, but it wasn't enough. There was this terrible restlessness gnawing away at my insides all the time. Do you know what I mean?'

There was something almost confiding about his tone now. All around the room came murmurs of agreement. 'You know the truth is, being human cannot be borne alone. We need help. Supernatural help. And don't be afraid of that word: that's what's available to us.' His voice rose excitedly, 'Supernatural help. For Jesus suffered the agony of being cut off from his Father for us. The way back to God is now open.'

John Morley stepped back while the boy came to life once more.

'Jesus,' he whispered, 'are you still there? Will you help me?'

And then a figure picked up all the boxes the boy had dropped, and said, 'I'm here. I'm with you. I'm never going to leave you.'

As the boy and Jesus left together Tara found herself moved. It was just a little bit of theatre, but something in it stirred her. Maybe it was the final words: 'I'm here. I'm with you. I'm never going to leave you.'

John Morley seemed moved, too. 'It's strange watching the greatest moment of your life; to experience again the extraordinary love of Jesus.' He seemed to say this more to himself than the audience. 'You see, with Jesus you will have a foundation to your life, you'll be putting your feet down on a rock, not the wobbly jelly the world offers you.'

Suddenly the woman who, earlier, had been breast-feeding her baby, stood up. 'I'm sorry,' she cried, 'but my seat has become very, very hot, I had to stand up.'

Katie nudged Tara. 'Looney alert,' she whispered. Tara nodded. She wished the woman would sit down again. She was only embarrassing herself – and Tara.

But if John Morley was irritated or shocked by this interruption he didn't show it. He just smiled courteously at the woman as if inviting her to continue.

'You see, I've got problems, like my little boy,' she nodded at the baby now sleeping in her arms. 'No, he's not the problem, I am. I've made mistakes. And I drink too much. But I can't seem to stop. I need Jesus's help. But how do I get it? Please tell me that.'

At once John Morley got down off the stage and came over to her. He smiled at the baby and murmured something. The woman replied, 'He's Martin and I'm Pauline.'

'Well, Pauline, do you believe that Jesus Christ can come into your life and transform it?'

She gazed up at him. 'Yes . . . Yes I do.'

'Then we're going to pray right now, Pauline, that he will do this for you.'

He took Pauline's hand in his and said a prayer. His voice was low and intimate, almost as if he were whispering in her ear. 'Now Pauline. You must pray and thank Jesus for hearing you and healing you.'

'Oh I hope so,' she began.

'Not hope so, he has,' said John Morley with quiet authority. Then very gently, 'Pauline, thank Jesus now for coming into your life.'

'All right,' she whispered. She stared upwards. 'Jesus, I've messed up my life good and proper. But I don't want it to be like this. Only you can help me, change it for me and my baby. So, thank you Jesus, from the bottom of my heart . . . thank you.'

At first Tara had cringed every time the woman spoke. She seemed like a character from one of those dire American chat shows, telling everything so indiscriminately you feel like a peeping Tom. But now Tara sensed the woman's total desperation; Jesus really was her only hope. And now Jesus was with her. Tara felt a sudden surge of excitement, and emotion.

Katie nudged her. 'You don't think this is a set-up, do you?'

'How do you mean?'

'Well, maybe this woman travels everywhere with him and does her little act . . .'

'Oh no,' said Tara firmly. 'It has to be genuine.'

John Morley ended by urging everyone to follow Pauline's example: 'Get right with God. To live without Jesus is to die without him. So come on, don't sit there like boiled haggis, do something tonight. Come and talk to me or have a chat with Mark, Lisa, Alice and Jake – you can't miss them parading around in their Something More T-shirts. Or, how about signing up for one of our Bible study groups . . . you see, there's no middle way with Jesus. You're either for him or against him. So come on, get involved *tonight*.'

All around Tara there were excited conversations; some people were hugging each other. And Tara felt a part of it. It was intoxicating. She got up. 'I want to tell John Morley about my vision.' She didn't hear Katie's reply as she rushed towards him.

But Olivia got there first. Tara couldn't hold back a pang of irritation. She heard Olivia saying, 'And this is my friend Mary. She's the one Paul said you might be able to help.'

'Certainly,' said John Morley, shaking hands with them both.

'Mary's pulled a muscle in her right arm and at night she's been waking up in agony, haven't you?'

Mary nodded gravely.

'Oh, I'm very sorry to hear that. Will you show me exactly where it hurts?' he sounded like a kindly doctor. Mary indicated the top of her shoulder. 'Now, I'm going to see if I can help you by saying a prayer.' He put his hand on her shoulder. 'Lord, please heal this girl. She's got a bad arm, so we pray it gets better and doesn't hurt any more. Thank you Lord. Amen.'

Tara had always thought so-called healings were deeply suspect; but he'd spoken so simply and sincerely, she couldn't help being impressed. 'How does it feel?' she asked Mary.

'It does feel different,' she trembled slightly. 'Warmer somehow. Better, I think.'

They edged away just as Paul appeared. He chatted to John Morley, whom he obviously knew quite well, and then turned to Tara, introducing her as his friend.

She glowed a little at that. Then someone called Paul's name, he turned away and it was just her with John Morley.

'What you said about receiving supernatural help,' began Tara, timidly, 'well, I had an experience like that.' He smiled reassuringly, as if to say, I'd love to hear about it. So she began to tell him about her vision. But she soon found herself faltering, for his relaxed grin had begun to stiffen. He'd stopped nodding in approval. She finished abruptly. 'And it was such a wonderful feeling.'

He considered for a moment, like a doctor unsure how to tell someone a bad diagnosis. 'That's very interesting, of course, but can I ask you to be a bit careful?'

'Yes,' whispered Tara.

'You see, a good feeling isn't going to teach you anything. We are emotional creatures, after all. What you've got to do is weigh it, take it to church and they will test your experience for you, all right.'

Tara didn't trust herself to speak.

'My advice to you is associate with Christian people, find out what God is about and join a Bible group, that's when you'll start learning.' He tapped her on the shoulder: 'Best of luck, Tara.'

'Thanks,' murmured Tara. Eyes smarting, she turned away to find a plate of food pushed in front of her.

'I just piled on everything,' said Katie. 'I wasn't sure what you wanted.'

She nibbled at the food while Katie rattled on about a boy who kept looking at her, then Paul joined them again. Tara went on nodding and smiling, but some of the happiness had gone out of her. John Morley had acted just like Matt and Katie, really. He thought there was something dodgy about her vision too. No wonder he'd looked at her so uneasily. No one understood. Except Paul. And maybe even he'd just pretended he did, so he could convert her.

Tara sat locked inside her own gloomy thoughts until it was time to leave. It was cold and damp outside. She buttoned her coat up tightly.

Paul was bristling with vigour; he'd obviously found the evening very inspiring. 'So what did you think of it all, then?' he asked.

It was Katie who replied: 'Well, some of it was quite impressive, I have to admit that. And that John Morley's a good speaker.'

'Isn't he, though,' agreed Paul.

'But I'll tell you what ruined it for me, it was the way he polluted his talk with threats, like at the end when he said, if you don't do what we say now, you're damned when you die.'

'Well, he wasn't exactly saying that,' began Paul, 'but you see, the Bible is quite clear . . .'

'Maybe it is,' interrupted Katie, 'but I didn't like all that bit about you're either in the gang or you're not.' She turned to Tara. 'You're very quiet, are you all right?' Paul was gazing anxiously at her too.

'Oh, I'm fine,' said Tara, 'just a bit tired, that's all.'

'Soon be home,' said Paul. 'Look, what you're saying is very interesting, Katie, perhaps we can talk about it in the car.' Conversation was difficult now as people were pouring out of the pubs. There were so many surging around the chip shop they had to walk in the road, dodging the large puddles.

Just ahead of them a small blonde girl was crying, 'Stop it, I don't want to go!' A man in a cherry-red suit had grabbed her by the arm, and she was trying to pull away from him. He was laughing and so was his mate in a garish blue suit beside him.

'Let go of me,' the girl's cry grew louder.

Tara averted her eyes; she hated watching a scene.

'Those guys are nothing but bullies,' she murmured softly to Katie.

They were already weaving past the girl when a familiar voice said, 'I think the lady wants to leave.' Paul was walking right up to the two men. Tara watched him, half-admiringly, half-fearfully. What was he getting into?

The men stared at Paul in astonishment. The one who had grabbed the girl so tightly snarled, 'Keep your big black nose out of it.'

'Yeah, come away Paul,' urged Katie.

But Paul didn't move. 'Let the lady go.' He reached forward to put a hand on the man's shoulder. '*Now.*'

The man was shocked into relaxing his hold on the girl. Seeing her chance she quickly ran away. She did not look back.

Paul took his hand away, but both men were circling him now. They were only a few centimetres shorter than him and one of them put his face right up to Paul. 'You're going to pay big for that.'

'Paul, come away,' cried Tara. But as she spoke Paul was punched in the face. Then, flying out of nowhere came two more men. They ran up behind Paul. One grabbed him by the neck, the other kicked furiously at the back of his legs.

Then Paul disappeared completely.

9 The Good Samaritan

They encircled Paul. Tara couldn't see what they were doing to him. But she could hear. They were kicking Paul as if he were not human, a thing they could safely vent their fury on.

He must be in agony now. She had to make them stop. She looked for Katie. She wasn't there. She must have fled. Tara was on her own. Her breath stopped.

Then, all at once she started screaming as if her life depended on it; a terrible piercing scream. 'Leave him alone!' she shrieked. And from behind her, like a deep echo, she heard, 'Leave him alone.'

Tara whirled round. Two large guys in white shirts and black bomber jackets were suddenly standing on the edge of the pavement. She felt a touch on her shoulder. It was Katie. 'I got the bouncers from the pub, they'll sort them out.' Her whisper felt hot on Tara's neck.

The bouncers didn't seem to be moving at all, making them eerily unreal, like the life-size cardboard cut-outs in cinema foyers. But their presence was enough. Paul's attackers were edging away. Caught in the pale, yellow street light, they looked grubby and dazed.

'He was asking for it,' whined one of them self-righteously.

The two bouncers lumbered forward and in a professional but distinctly impersonal way helped Paul to his feet. They muttered something to him, then resumed their spot at the end of the pavement, like two sentries.

Blood was streaming down Paul's face. He staggered forward. Tara thought he looked as if he'd escaped from a horror film. He could hardly stand up. She clasped hold of one hand, Katie took hold of the other hand: 'How do you feel?' she whispered.

'I've felt better,' he spluttered. He'd been turned into this gasping, bleeding ruin, but even now he was trying to make a feeble joke of it; it was almost unbearable.

In a blind rage she yelled at Paul's attackers: 'Look what you've done . . . you . . . you're animals . . . no, you're less than animals, you're the lowest form of life there is . . . you haven't got one brain cell between the four of you. You're . . . you're . . .' there were no words terrible enough for them. But murmurs of support for her came from the gathering crowd.

'Those blokes have been causing trouble all evening,' cried a woman. The blokes in question were edging further and further away but still grumbling, 'He started it.'

'Could someone call an ambulance,' Tara shouted.

'It's all right, we've done that.' A man with a grey beard rushed forward in his coat and slippers. He was carrying a chair: 'My wife's bringing a blanket.'

Paul slumped on to the chair with a sigh. He struggled to say thank you, then he sat forward with his shoulders hunched like an old, old man.

Tara knelt beside him. A woman bustled forward with a blanket, which she carefully placed round Paul.

'Oh, thank you, thank you,' cried Tara. 'Did they say how long the ambulance would be?'

'They'll be as fast as they can, love,' said the woman. 'We told them it was an emergency . . . I'll nip back and get a cloth for his head. I'd get him a hot drink too, but I'd better not in case he's got to be operated on.' She rushed off while the man with the grey beard smiled reassuringly at Tara and Katie.

'We live just over the newsagent's there,' he pointed down the road. 'We see this sort of thing happen so often. We admire what you did, young man, but it's best not to get involved. You'll get no thanks for it, you know.'

Paul didn't reply, then the woman returned and applied a cold compress to Paul's head and gave him a pad to hold under his nose, which was still bleeding. She stayed with him until the ambulance roared urgently into view.

Then everything was a blur of activity as Paul was helped on to a stretcher and more and more people jostled around for a gawp. Tara spotted Olivia in the crowd; she seemed genuinely shaken. But there was no time to say anything to her. Inside the ambulance Katie looked at Tara dazedly a couple of times as if to say, is this real?

Paul lay with a pad over his nose. He kept trying to move. 'Does your head hurt very much?' asked Tara.

'No, I'm just trying to stop it spinning away,' he replied in such a weak voice, it was like a knife going through Tara.

Paul was rushed into casualty. Tara and Katie were ushered into a tiny waiting-room. There was no one else there. Tara got them both a cup of coffee from the machine, but neither of them could drink it.

'I don't believe tonight,' cried Katie suddenly. 'I mean, one minute we're all talking about how much Jesus loves us and the next Paul's being beaten up by a bunch of thugs and you're screaming . . . I've never heard you scream like that before.'

'It was so lucky you got those bouncers,' said Tara.

'They didn't want to come, said they never got involved in street violence. They were quite snooty about it. It was only when I started getting hysterical that they followed me out. I can't even remember what I said to them.' Her voice tightened. 'And do you know what's the worst of it? That girl who Paul helped, the one who caused all this, did a runner.'

'She was probably terrified,' said Tara.

'Or maybe she's back with the guy in that awful red suit laughing with him about her Good Samaritan . . . I suppose it is pretty funny.' She gave a kind of crazy laugh which turned into a sob.

Tara held her while she cried. She stroked Katie's hair and whispered how it was going to be all right, which seemed to soothe her; in a way, it soothed Tara as well. Then they sat huddled together until the nurse appeared, briskly telling them how they'd put six stitches over Paul's right eye, packed his nose and given him some painkillers. Now they were x-raying his knees.

Tara rang her grandparents. There was a sharp intake of breath from her nan, followed by, 'Don't worry, we'll be there right away.' When they did arrive Tara was almost ashamed at how relieved she was to see them; she could let them take charge now.

Then Olivia and her parents appeared, eager to help, and everyone stood around talking and sympathising about Paul's plight, except for Katie, who was crouched in the corner half asleep.

Finally they were allowed to see Paul. There was an awkward silence for a moment; Tara felt suddenly self-conscious with her grandparents there. Then Grandad called out, 'What were you doing then, trying to be a dead hero?' It was a rather uncertain joke, but Paul smiled anyway, then Nan gave him a hug, muttering, 'What kind of world do we live in?'

As Paul was helped into Grandad's car, Tara wondered what he thought about tonight. He must be regretting what he'd done – getting caught up in other people's ugliness. It had been a totally futile gesture, yet it stirred Tara.

Next day the house was awhirl with activity. First the police arrived to take statements (against the advice of Tara and her grandparents, Paul didn't wish to press charges). Olivia came with her parents, who had driven Paul's car back. Two people Tara recognised from last night's meeting also arrived. A reporter and photographer from the local press came to photograph Paul in bed with a Rescue Rayner badge pinned to his pyjamas. The district nurse told Paul he couldn't even think about returning to work until Wednesday at the earliest, when the stitches would be taken out. She also told Nan that Paul needed a light diet with lots of nourishing fluids.

This was Tara's cue to race up and down with hot drinks, scrambled eggs on toast, milk shakes . . . She was just on her way up the stairs with a mug of tea when the doorbell rang.

'Answer that, will you dear,' called Nan. 'I've got the oven door open.'

Tara expected to see Katie, instead, it was her father. 'Forgot my key,' he began, then, seeing the cup of tea, 'Is that for me?'

Tara smiled faintly at his little joke. 'So how are you?' he asked.

'A bit busy,' said Tara, briskly. 'Do you want Nan? she's in the kitchen.'

'I wanted to talk to you both, because actually, I've got a little bit of good news.' Tara shifted impatiently. Was this man, hovering so uncertainly like a door-to-door salesman on his first day, really her dad? Even now, she still waited for him to be exposed as an imposter.

'I've been going after this job selling computer software. Anyway, there were two interviews and the upshot is, I've got the job. I'll hear officially tomorrow, but someone rang me this morning to put me out of my misery. It's a French company, actually, get a car thrown in as well . . .' he looked at Tara for some kind of positive reaction.

But she was in a state of panic. Did his job mean Nan and Grandad wouldn't need a lodger any more, wouldn't need Paul? 'Well, I hope it works out,' she said, more ungenerously than she'd intended. But it would be just like him to say that now he was earning money again Paul could leave at the end of the month. 'There's a high turnover in sales jobs, isn't there?' she said. 'It's not very secure, is it?'

'They seem quite keen to have me.'

'That's something, I suppose,' she conceded grudgingly.

'Anyway, am I allowed inside?' He was becoming irritated now and adopting that slightly mocking, superior tone Tara always loathed.

He stared at her, trying to change gear. 'Look, Tara, what I wanted to say was, as a little celebration I'd like to take you out for a meal, just you and me, go where you want . . .' he smiled hopefully at her.

'Thanks, but I'm pretty busy with school – just started my GCSEs and I can't really afford the time . . .' she faltered. He didn't seem to know what to say either. The silence between them was like a cry.

'Well, I'd better take this tea up before it gets cold,' she said, finally.

'Yes, yes,' he said absently. 'Who's it for, anyway?'

'Paul, he got injured helping someone last night.'

Before he could reply Nan appeared. 'Oh, I thought I heard your voice. What a lovely surprise. Well, don't stand in the doorway like that . . .'

Tara fled upstairs. She darted into her room, squirted some perfume into the air, then walked into it; she'd read in a magazine that was how you were supposed to put on perfume. Then she knocked on Paul's door. She still couldn't hold back a little shiver of excitement. And she'd been inside Paul's bedroom so often today.

He was propped up in bed. His face was swollen and his eyes looked dull and without their usual brightness. But he seemed in good spirits. 'I brought you some tea. Hope it's not gone cold.'

He took a sip, 'Just how I like it.' His voice became confiding: 'Will you do me a favour?' She sat down on the edge of his bed, then stared at him eagerly.

'The doctor says I shouldn't go back to work until Wednesday. But tomorrow's a crucial day as you know. My friend is coming in to do a feature on the school for the telly, so I can't miss that. Yet, your nan's saying I go back to work over her dead body . . .'

'That's my nan for you.'

'I know and she's a top person but . . . will you have a word with her, tell her I'm much better?'

'You're not, though. You're still recovering.'

He raised his hand dismissively. 'I thought, at least, *you*'d be on my side,' he said lightly.

'I am and I'm not.'

'A kind of double-agent: Mata Tara.'

She smiled and in the same easy tone said, 'If you will go around rescuing young damsels, what do you expect? Paul, why did you do it?'

He grimaced. 'A good question.'

'I mean, if you'd just looked the other way, you wouldn't be lying here now, would you?'

'That's true.'

Her question still hung in the air.

'Do you really want to know?' he asked, quite shyly.

'Yes,' replied Tara fervently. 'But only if you want to tell me.'

He stretched out and picked up the Bible, which was the only thing on his bedside table. 'Now, there's a section in Matthew . . . here we are. Jesus says, "When I was hungry you gave me food, when I was thirsty you gave me drink, when I was a stranger you took me into your home, when naked you clothed me, when I was ill you came to my help, when in prison you visited me," and the people say to him, "but Jesus, when did we do all these things?" and Jesus replies, "I tell you this, anything you did for one of my brothers here, however humble, you did for me." ' He paused, then added simply, 'I can't turn my back on Jesus.'

'All right . . . No, that's an impossible thing to ask,' she declared. 'How can you treat everybody as if they were Jesus? What about all the horrible, nasty people? They do exist, Paul.'

He shrugged. 'Jesus is quite clear on this point: "If a man says he loves God and hates his brother he is a liar." '

'Yes, but . . . how could anyone do that?'

'Look, we're all miserable sinners. On my own I couldn't do it for five minutes, but with God's help,' his face lit up, 'anything is possible.'

'Anything is possible,' repeated Tara. 'In that case . . . Paul, will you answer me a direct question?'

'Sure.'

'Do you believe my vision was from God? Because John Morley doesn't,' she added fiercely.

'Look, I expect John was just being careful. You see, lots of people claim to see things. Look at all those people who are totally convinced they've seen flying saucers.'

'And been abducted by sex-starved aliens.'

'Exactly. Anyway, John doesn't know you as I do.'

'That's true,' said Tara, softly.

'I believe your vision is leading you towards God – and that's the only real test.' He suddenly sank back.

'Am I tiring you?'

'No, this is food and drink to me,' Paul said fervently. 'I'll just rest my eyes for a moment, but carry on talking, please.'

'OK . . . what I find hard to believe about it all . . . well why would God take all that trouble over me?'

'Tara, if you magnified the most wonderful human love a million times you still couldn't describe God's love for us, for you.'

'So you think maybe that light was God saying to me, "I care about you . . . I love you," ' she faltered.

Paul opened his eyes. 'I know that's what it was.'

Tara shivered. 'It's wonderful, but a bit scary too, all this divine help suddenly pouring out of the sky.' She half-laughed: 'If I did become a Christian, what exactly would I have to do?'

'A Christian is someone who believes in Jesus with their head and their whole heart and through Jesus makes a commitment to God . . . and makes him Lord of their Life and . . .' he half-chanted these words as if he'd said them many, many times before, but then he said, 'Before I was a Christian I was just that kid from the home. People either treated me as a nobody or were full of sympathy, which I did not want. But in God's eyes we're all special, we're all valuable . . . I can't tell you what a difference that has made to my life.'

He smiled sheepishly. 'When you feel yourself tottering off in a small doze, let me know.'

'No, it's really interesting.'

His eyes glittered. 'Really?'

'Yes, really. So come on, tell me, what's my next step?'

'OK, why don't you come along to one of the Christian Union meetings at Rayner? You'd be very welcome.'

Tara swallowed hard. She'd peeked in the window at a couple of Christian Union meetings, there were only a handful of pupils there and none of them were . . . It sounded awfully snobby, but in the school pecking order they were right at the bottom: sad, shy people who were grateful if you even said hello to them. Tara couldn't see herself sitting in the middle of them.

'Well, yes, I might do that,' she murmured unenthusiastically.

'I know everyone there would be really pleased to see you.' She was sure they would. She could just picture them with their creepy smiles: 'Hello, Tara, we want to be your friend.'

'Yes, well maybe,' said Tara, desperately trying to change the subject. 'But I was thinking more of . . .' Paul looked at her questioningly, '. . . of things like initiation ceremonies.'

'Initiation ceremonies,' he repeated.

'Yes, do you have any of those to be a Christian?'

'We certainly do,' said Paul, solemnly. 'There are different ones for men and women actually. The women have to carry a headless chicken for one kilometre, while the men . . . it's really tough for them. They have to slip a live scorpion down their trousers.'

'But that's . . .' began Tara indignantly, and then she saw Paul's face. 'You really had me going there.'

Paul couldn't answer, he'd rolled his head back and was roaring with laughter. Whenever he laughed he was just like a big kid again.

'I'm sorry — I couldn't resist it,' he spluttered. 'Your face.' Now both of them had collapsed into laughter.

'You sound very happy in here.' Tara's dad hovered in the doorway.

Tara wiped her eyes. 'It's just something Paul said,' she gasped.

Her dad smiled uncertainly. 'So how are you, Paul?'

Tara watched Paul trying to assume a serious expression; that nearly sent her off again.

'Hey, I'm much better, thanks, good as new.'

'Don't believe him,' said Nan, bustling in with some antibiotic tablets. 'He has to take these every four hours, although if I weren't here I'm sure he'd forget.'

Then Grandad appeared. 'I found a shop that was open,' he said to Nan, 'and I got all the things on your list.'

Before Nan could reply Tara's dad was exclaiming, 'Hello, Dad, what are you doing here? Isn't it one of your steam train excursions today?'

Tara's dad was right; in fact, Tara had planned to accompany her grandad on this trip. She always enjoyed the excursions. Her grandad was at his most relaxed and Tara loved it when he would point at a steam train puffing away and solemnly intone, 'Tara, that train is breathing with the fire of life.'

'Yes, I was due to go to Brighton with Tara,' said Grandad, in that oddly formal way in which he always addressed Tara's dad. 'But due to the exploits of this brave fool . . .' a note of genuine affection entered his voice, '. . . I've had to cancel.'

'Well, I don't know,' replied Tara's dad. 'And I thought steam train excursions were sacred.' There was no mistaking the bitterness in his voice.

Tara could even spare her dad a pinch of sympathy. After all, his good news had been completely submerged by Paul's latest exploit. But then, whose fault was that? It was her dad who'd written himself out of this family. He didn't deserve any better treatment. She watched him walk towards his car, hurrying, head bowed, slightly stooped, a sense of strain about him. For one crazy moment she even found herself worrying about him, wondering where he would go next. Then he disappeared into the frail, autumn light.

She doubted if they'd see him again for some time.

10 Rayner lives

Next day the news of Paul's act of bravery swept through the school. Tara and Katie were inundated with questions. And the events of Saturday night seemed to grow more dramatic each time they told them.

As Paul's representative, Tara was also flooded with get-well cards, messages and boxes of chocolates: 'I'm going to need a truck to take all these home,' she exclaimed.

Matt, of course, was vastly amused by it all. 'We'll all sleep sounder in our beds tonight, knowing good old Paul is out there righting wrongs on our streets. I can picture it now: "Sir, I find the way you are looking at that young damsel's left eyebrow quite reprehensible. So this is the night appointed to let you beat me up." '

But Matt was a lone dissenter. And in the afternoon, when the school was assembling outside for the TV crew, people kept coming up to Tara saying what a shame it was that Paul couldn't be here.

And suddenly, there he was, walking slowly towards them, leaning on one of Grandad's sticks, with Nan and Grandad either side of him.

Tara dashed over.

'He's even more determined than your grandmother,' said Grandad. 'And that's saying something.'

'He'll probably catch his death of cold out here,' declared Nan, 'but I . . . warned him.'

It was certainly freezing this afternoon; in fact, Tara's face was burning with the cold. While they were waiting for the cameraman Tara was introduced to Gavin, Paul's contact. He wore wire-rimmed glasses, a casually unbuttoned waistcoat and a brown jacket. He seemed to share Paul's sense of humour and enthusiasm. At one point Gavin turned to Tara confidingly and said, 'Poor old Paul looks pretty frail, doesn't he?'

'We told him not to come today, but he insisted.'

'He lives with you, doesn't he?'

'Well, yes,' began Tara.

'Keep an eye on him for me, will you?'

Tara nodded solemnly. 'Of course I will.'

'Thanks.' He smiled at her. Tara felt as if she was about twenty-two – and Paul's girlfriend.

At last the cameraman arrived. He and Gavin started interviewing some of the pupils, who were on their honour not to mention that they'd had to wear hats and scarves in some classrooms today because the heating had broken down.

Then Gavin approached Tara, Katie and Matt: 'I'm sure we'll get some lively views here.' He signalled to the cameraman who came over. 'Now, when I ask you a question look at me, not at the camera, when you answer. OK?' He grinned at Katie, 'And relax, all right?'

'All right,' gasped Katie.

'Now the council says it can't afford to keep your school open, what do you say?'

Tara dived in: 'This is the village school, many people's grand-parents came here. It's a good school too, if only the council would give it a chance. But money always comes first . . . It's our playing-field it really wants. The biggest playing-field for over seventy-five kilometres, you know.'

'And of course, the councillors,' added Matt, 'would steal the elastic out of their grandmothers' knickers if they could sell it at a profit.'

Gavin looked questioningly at Katie who said, 'Some people's grandparents came here, you know . . . oh, you've already said that, haven't you Tara? Sorry.' Covered in confusion, she stopped.

'Well, that's super,' said Gavin, who'd been nodding and smiling all the time they were talking. 'Thank you very much.' He and the cameraman set off in the direction of the headmaster.

'I really messed that up,' said Katie. 'But I was shaking inside.' Matt gave her hand an affectionate squeeze.

Finally came the big crowd scene: staff and pupils forming one giant semicircle round the school.

'Come on, get closer, closer,' urged Gavin.

'Now, I'm going to ask you, if your school should stay open, and I want you to yell, "Yes," as loud as you can: Ready . . .?' Gavin asked the question and his face lit up with pleasure as the deafening reply came back to him. Then with a few handshakes and a pat on the back to Paul, he and the cameraman raced off, as they were hoping to use that story on tonight's local news.

'Our school's going to be famous,' yelled one boy. The older pupils laughed indulgently. But there was a feeling that Rayner School was off the ropes and fighting back.

'Would you like to go home now, Paul?' asked Tara.

'Yes I would,' he said quickly.

But before Tara could attract her grandparents' attention, Olivia rushed over with Mary.

'Paul, Mary's got something to tell you.'

Mary smiled nervously at Paul. 'I just wanted to tell you . . . you know my right arm was paining, so John Morley said a prayer? Well, it's not hurting any more. The pain's completely gone.'

'Hey, that's wonderful,' said Paul with some of his old vigour.

'I still can't believe it,' said Mary.

'We didn't think those things happened any more,' said Olivia.

Paul beamed around at them all. 'Oh yes, they certainly do. I mean, only the other week I was watching a video of this woman in a wheelchair who couldn't walk. The preacher said, "In the name of Jesus Christ, walk," and she just got up and ran off. And he said, "Where is she? Where has she gone?" She was running around crying, "I can walk. I can walk." Now she plays the saxophone in the church choir every Sunday.' His voice rang with conviction. 'And these are registered stories.'

'That's absolutely amazing,' declared Matt. His tone sounded sincere yet the expression on his face was mocking. 'So does that mean, Paul, you'll be running about, fully restored to health, tomorrow?'

Paul smiled regretfully. 'It doesn't quite work like that.'

'Pity, pity,' sighed Matt, then he looked significantly at Tara.

At half-past six, Katie, Tara, Paul and her grandparents were all in the sitting-room watching the local news. Other news stories rambled past while they waited with growing impatience for their spot. Finally, at four minutes to seven the announcer said, 'It's been their village school for over sixty years, but now the council wants to close it, Gavin Wilkins reports from Rayner School.'

There were some shots of the village, ending with a longer shot of the school, and a local declaring, 'Close Rayner and you tear the heart out of this village.' The headmaster and a governor spoke about the school's value to the community, then the picture switched to Tara, Matt and Katie. All that was left of Tara's speech was, 'It's the playing-fields they want,' but Matt's comments were shown in full.

One of the councillors appeared to loud boos from everyone in Tara's sitting-room. He was a pasty-faced individual in a crumpled, pin-striped suit. He said the closure of Rayner School was regrettable, but it just wasn't financially viable to keep it open.

'What nonsense,' replied Nan. 'And did you notice the gravy stains all down his tie?'

The report ended all too quickly with the cameraman pulling back for the shot of everyone standing together outside the school and that great roar of 'Yes!'

They played back the report several times on the video. Finally, Grandad declared, 'You did very well, Paul. The council won't like that piece at all. But it's not enough, we need something more. Someone with a bit of power on our side.'

After the elation of seeing their school on the news, they came back down to earth again. Grandad was right: they couldn't win on their own.

That night Tara prayed for Rayner School.

Years ago she used to pray a lot, or rather, she made bargains with God. It started with a maths exam she was terrified of failing. In desperation, she told God if he helped her pass the exam she would donate ten of her books to the new charity bookshop.

When she passed the exam she somewhat grudgingly fulfilled her part of the deal. She made similar deals with God over the next few months. In the end her bookshelves were becoming alarmingly depleted, so she decided to go it alone.

But tonight was different. She closed her eyes and pictured the light she'd seen. Paul's words came back to her: 'If you magnified the most wonderful human love a million times you still couldn't describe God's love for us.'

To think of God, the creator of the universe, caring about her, and wanting to help her. She began to understand why Paul was always talking about his faith.

It was the most wonderful, amazing revelation. And it meant there was no need to barter with God. She remembered how simply John Morley had spoken when he was asking God to heal Olivia's friend, Mary. So finally she said, 'God, Rayner is a very good school. Please help us to keep it open. Thank you.'

As she reflected on her prayer, a wonderful feeling of peace came over her. She drifted off to sleep and then she woke up, or rather, half woke up. She seemed to be in that strange world, halfway between dreams and waking.

There was a sense of warmth all around her.

And then a voice reached her. It was inside her head and yet it seemed to reverberate around the room too.

'Rayner lives,' it said.

11 Matt's warning

'And that was all I heard, just those two words: "Rayner lives",' said Tara. She was sitting in a semicircle with the rest of the Christian Union group; on all their faces was a look of intense concentration.

'Sometimes after I've been praying for a long time I'll hear a voice in my head,' said a girl called Catherine. 'And I think, can that be God speaking to me?' She turned to Paul, 'Is that possible?'

'Oh yes, Catherine,' cried Paul. 'What about those words from Genesis when it speaks of "hearing the voice of God walking in the garden in the cool of the day''?' A sharp thrill ran through the whole room: to think of God so close, so reachable.

'I just want you to know that what you said has really helped me,' said another girl with a brace on her teeth, whose name Tara hadn't caught, 'you see, my parents want me to leave Rayner at Christmas. They say it will be less disruptive. But now I can tell them: Rayner lives. Thank you, Tara.' There were murmurs of agreement.

Tara gave a guilty smile. She'd dreaded this meeting. Right up to the last moment she didn't think she could attend. Especially when Katie refused point-blank to go with her: 'I thought the meeting we went to with Paul was interesting but I don't want to go to any more. I do believe in God but in my own way and I don't want anyone else – not even Paul – telling me I'm wrong and I'm damned. I hate all that side of it. Sorry Tara, but there it is.'

In the end Tara prayed for advice: should she go to that Bible class alone? At first the usual arguments whirled around her head, and then a strange calmness came over her and into her head dropped a memory.

It was Tara's first week at Rayner School. Teams were being picked for netball, and she was the very last one to be chosen. They never even said her name.

Even now she could taste that humiliation. After one week at school she'd been categorised as the lowest of the low. An outcast. A joke.

During the netball game Tara almost knocked herself out, she tried so hard. And her rating went up a little after that. But it was her friendship with madcap, likeable Katie which really clinched it. And in the early days it was Tara who'd done all the running in that relationship.

She'd worked hard for her popularity. And she was determined to cling on to it. For there were still moments when she feared she'd be found out; that everyone would discover she wasn't very different from the sad people at these meetings. Deep down Tara knew she was just as intense and eager to please, and geekish, as they were.

And if she started associating with them – well then her cover would be blown.

In a flash Tara understood it all. And at the same time she felt almost recklessly brave: now she could challenge her fear.

For she knew that moment of revelation had come from God. He'd answered her prayer in the most wonderful way. Tara was so lucky to be able to draw on this supernatural power whenever she wanted.

And in the end, sitting in the Christian Union meeting was a breeze. She could even smile back at Matt and Katie, and some of her other friends when they made faces through the window at her for 'sitting with the gormos'. There were nine of them at the meeting with her: all second and third years, eight of them girls. Tara could recognise herself in every one of them.

Catherine asked Paul if they could say a prayer for their school.

'Of course,' said Paul. 'But don't underestimate your own personal prayers, will you, because prayer is the most powerful form of energy we can generate – and after you've prayed you'll see doors opening up everywhere. You won't believe it.'

Then Tara, like everyone else, closed her eyes and heard Paul say,

'Thank you Lord for Jesus Christ, who took away all our sins and thank you for today and its joys. We pray for your help Lord, so that everyone in this school will work together and that it will not close. Amen.'

After the meeting finished Paul said, 'They were all so happy to see you . . . and so was I.'

'Yeah, the group's in double figures now, thanks to me,' said Tara, lightly.

'That's it, now I can retire a happy man. I suppose you want a lift home.'

'Of course.'

'All right if I stop off in town first? I've ordered a plant for your nan as a little thank you.'

'Oh she'll love that.'

Paul pulled up right beside the flower shop. 'Bit of luck getting a space so near . . . won't be long.' For a moment his face contorted with pain as he clambered out of the car; he said that was when his knees hurt the most. Tara watched him hobble into the flower shop. About two minutes later he reappeared with what Tara identified as Nan's plant in one hand and a bunch of pink bud roses in the other. He walked slowly towards her. He was smiling rather nervously.

'I got your nan an azalea. And I got you these, as a small thank you.' He almost threw the pink roses at her.

'But, for what?' she exclaimed.

'For that night.'

'All I did was scream.'

'Anyway, you deserve them.'

Tara had a horrible feeling she was going to burst into tears. 'But they're beautiful, my favourite.'

He smiled and carefully got back into the car.

'I've never had flowers before,' she said. 'Not ever.'

'I'm glad,' he replied, 'because every time in the future when you're given flowers – all those hundreds of times – you'll still remember me. The very first.'

She sniffed her flowers. Their fragrance made her quite faint with happiness. Then, as Paul was starting up the car, she cried out, 'Do we have to go back yet?' Going home was like returning to her cage. And she wanted to fly, to soar, just for a little while longer.

'How about if we have a quick cuppa somewhere?' A crazy suggestion, as the first thing Nan would do when they got home was make a pot of tea.

But Paul readily agreed. They walked up the main high street to the tea rooms. As soon as they entered they were assaulted by the warm, sickly scent of hot chocolate, toast and coffee. Then Tara exchanged the briefest of nods with one of the waitresses. She let out a sigh.

'What's the matter?' asked Paul.

'Just seen someone I know – well very vaguely – Annette something, goes to Priestley, Matt liked her but she messed him about. Now she's trying to get back with him, or so Katie reckons.'

Annette whirled past them in her white shirt and black skirt, carrying a tray of disgusting-looking pastries. 'Hope she doesn't serve us,' said Tara. They sat down, Tara handed Paul a menu. 'This is on me. I insist.'

'We'll see,' replied Paul.

A few moments later a male voice several feet above her asked, 'Are you ready to order?' She froze in her chair. All the noise in the tea room seemed to die away. She gripped her menu tightly. Now Paul was ordering something. But all she heard was his question to her at the end: 'What would you like?'

'Same as you,' she croaked.

Then slowly she looked up. For a moment Phil blocked out everything else. She took a deep breath. And another. But from him not a flicker of recognition. Total blankness. And that still wounded. All Tara could do was let the pain twist inside her. But it quickly faded; just a splinter there now. She watched him walk away; she felt oddly calm but strange, then she turned to Paul who was watching her anxiously.

'Hey, where are you?'

'I'm sorry.'

'What's wrong?'

She tried to explain. It was so bizarre, so totally unexpected it was almost comical now. 'That guy who served us, that was Phil.'

'Phil,' echoed Paul, and then a flicker of recognition crossed his face. 'Do you want to leave? Because we can go somewhere else.'

She was breathless for some reason. 'No . . . I'm fine here . . . anyway, if we left it would make him feel too important.'

'Sssh, he's coming back,' said Paul.

'A pot of tea for two,' he announced. 'And scones and jam for two.' Two trays were expertly placed on the table.

'That's six pounds eighty, please,' he said.

'I'll get this,' announced Tara.

'No, hold on . . .' began Paul.

'Honestly Paul, I insist. You've just bought me those lovely flowers.' Her voice was ringing out across the tea room now. Paul obviously understood and didn't argue. 'There you are, six pounds eighty exactly,' she said. 'But I'm forgetting your tip.' And with a brief smile she handed him a fifty pence tip.

Did his hand shake as he took the money from her? Oh, at least let his hand shake.

She permitted herself one final look at Phil in his newly pressed white shirt and black trousers. Of all the places to find him, a genteel tea room would be one of the very last. Still, he probably needed the money. When she knew him he was always broke.

When she knew him. What a strange phrase. As if knowing someone was something you could switch on and off. Still, she was better off without him now. At last even she knew that was true. Yet questions still burned inside her: why did he do it? How could he just cut her off like a dead branch? Did he feel smothered by her? Or maybe he thought she knew too much about him? Or did he just become bored?

If only she could creep inside his mind, although maybe the answer wasn't even there. She would never know. Still, she was certain of one thing now: his hand really did shake when she gave him the money.

Tara turned to Phil and gave a rather exaggerated laugh. 'I don't know, why is seeing one's ex always so messy?'

'I thought you carried it off very well.'

'Thanks, how about your ex, has she been in touch since her last visit?'

Paul raised his eyes. 'Sent me a card, on which she'd adapted this line from Shakespeare. It just said, "And if you love me not, chaos is come again," ' he frowned. 'I didn't even try to answer that one. I can't cope with all that stuff.' He made a face and suddenly became all schoolboyish.

'And there's no one else?' This was a bit cheeky of her to ask, but Paul didn't seem to take offence. Instead, he gazed right at her. 'Hans Solo, that's me.'

That evening as she arranged his flowers in a vase she thought again of what Paul had said: 'Hans Solo.' Did that mean he was lonely? She rather suspected he was. Something in her leapt at the idea. She would look after him, she would take away his loneliness.

She put the flowers by her mum's picture. If only her mum could see those flowers now; she'd understand just how beautiful they were.

Outside, snow was flurrying against the window. The first snow of winter; she always loved that. In days past she, Katie and Matt would have gone charging out and had a massive snowball fight. But tonight the snow had another significance; it seemed to put an even greater distance between those warm, mellow, spring-like days when she'd gone out with Phil, and the stifling hot summer she'd wasted mourning him. Let the snow bury him completely now.

The doorbell rang. It was Matt.

He bowed slightly. 'Fancy a walk in the snow?'

'Yes, sure,' she began, then stopped. Matt was smiling at her and yet he wasn't. 'How are you?' she asked cautiously as they set off together, their boots crunching through the snow.

'I'm OK,' he said shortly.

It was cold, their breath smoked every time they spoke. 'I want it a lot deeper than this,' said Matt. 'I like it when the snow brings everything to a halt.'

'But even this is good, Matt, all those bare, dead trees suddenly covered in whiteness, new life.'

'Now don't go all poetic on me – and anyway, that "new life" as you call it will just be a puddle of dirty slush in a couple of days.' He said this so fiercely, so bitterly.

'What's wrong?' Tara asked at once.

He gave a shuddering sigh. 'Do you really want to know?'

'Yes, of course.'

'You – you're the problem.'

'Me?'

'Yeah, I don't know why I bother with you.'

'Oh, Matt,' cried Tara, genuinely stunned by this outburst. 'What have I done? Tell me.'

He walked a little way from her, then over his shoulder he said, 'You were seen.'

'You mean in the Christian Union meeting? But I told you . . .'

'No, no,' he interrupted brusquely. 'Out having an intimate cup of tea with your . . . the lodger with muscles.'

'Who told you?'

'What does it matter?'

'It was Annette, wasn't it? The little stirrer.'

He shrugged his shoulders. 'Not denying it then . . . and he bought you some flowers.'

'Eavesdropping as well, was she?'

'She said she couldn't help hearing, you were shouting it out.'

'And did she mention that Phil, my unbeloved ex, was there too, serving?'

'She did, as it happens. Must have been quite an interesting situation for you.'

Tara stared at Matt indignantly. 'What your spy didn't tell you is that Paul bought my nan flowers too, as a thank you for looking after him, that's what mine were for. Honestly, the nerve of that girl spreading rumours, especially after all the things I've heard about her . . . I really hate her.'

'That's not a very Christian thing to say.' There was no mistaking the mockery in his voice.

'Matt, you can be so horrible sometimes.'

'Only sometimes? I'm slipping.'

Tara managed a small smile. 'She's really wound you up, hasn't she?'

'No, it's not her,' he turned away again.

'What do you mean?'

123

He picked up a piece of snow and made as if to aim it at Tara, then threw it hard against a tree. 'The snow's stopping,' he announced. 'Shame.' Then he looked at Tara and said, quite kindly, 'I don't want to see you mess up again.'

'What do you mean?'

'Tara, he's your teacher, he's ten years older than you . . .'

'I know. I know.'

'So what are you doing?'

Her voice rose. 'Look, I had a cup of tea with him, he bought Nan and me some flowers to thank us for looking after him, that's all . . .' She practically screamed the last two words at him.

'What about all this Christianity lark then?'

'OK, I'm interested in Christianity. Very interested.'

'Because he is.'

'No . . .'

'Oh, don't lie,' he said wearily. 'You're just like those women who go to church every Sunday because they've got a crush on the vicar.'

They glowered at each other. She was angry and irritated with Matt. She was tempted to say something hard and crushing. But then she saw him. His nose had turned bright red. And his eyes were wide and full of pain.

'Matt,' she whispered, 'I hate it when we argue. And I don't even know what we're arguing about . . . I mean, there's nothing wrong with being interested in Christianity, is there?'

'No,' he agreed cautiously. She could sense a 'but' hovering there. She nodded at him as if to say, go on.

'Well, don't get mad, but I think Christians tend to hook people who are a bit confused.'

'Like me?'

He smiled wolfishly. 'Especially you.'

'Oh, thanks.'

'Katie's told me a bit about it; how you've got to surrender your life to God and you mustn't think for yourself, you've got to do what the Bible says.'

'That's not . . .' began Tara.

But Matt swept on. 'And all this getting down on your knees and whipping yourself with barbed-wire because of your sins: I once danced to Status Quo, forgive me . . . forgive me.'

Tara shook her head. 'You've got it all wrong.'

He turned away from her.

'No, come on,' she cried. 'Let me have my say now.'

'Go on, then.'

'Look, it's hard to explain.'

'Oh, what a shame.'

'No, listen, it's as if before I had blinkers on and . . .'

'And now the blinkers are off?' interrupted Matt. 'Wow, that's amazing, Tara.'

Tara was half-laughing, half-frustrated now. She wiped some snow from her face. 'When I saw that light it was as if a door had sprung open. Now I want to find out where that door is leading to. Is that so wrong?'

She waited for Matt to make another crack, but he didn't. He stood staring at her, then said, suddenly, 'All right, I'll tell you something. About a year ago I was sitting on a train, all on my own, coming back from my uncle's, when for no reason I felt incredibly happy. It was the weirdest feeling, it was as if everything just came together and I thought, being alive is pretty good really. What's totally amazing is I hadn't drunk anything either.'

Tara said slowly, 'Matt, where do you think that feeling came from?'

'From somewhere inside me. I don't know why it popped up then. But I created it.'

'So, won't you even consider the possibility that maybe it was God reaching out to you?'

He shook his head vigorously.

'Why won't you just come to a meeting with me?'

'I'd rather stick with the soap powder I've got, thanks. You see, I'm just a doomed realist.' He smiled rather sadly, then said, 'All I'm asking, Tara, is don't go out with that Paul geezer again.'

'Oh, we're back to him, are we?'

'Yes we are, because . . . well your trouble is, you're looking for someone who doesn't exist. First of all there was this Phil character who had you believing all sorts of things about himself which weren't true.'

'All right, all right,' retorted Tara impatiently.

'And now you're doing exactly the same with your teacher.'

'He's not my teacher,' said Tara.

Matt shook his head. 'That's very revealing.'

'What, saying he's not my teacher?'

126

His voice tightened. 'Just answer me this then, how would you feel if you went home and saw Paul snuggling up to a girl?'

'He hasn't got a girlfriend,' said Tara at once.

'And would it matter to you, if he had?'

Tara hesitated.

'That's all I wanted to hear,' cried Matt.

'But let me . . .'

'No need,' he shouted. 'That said it all. Go on then, chase after the guy who's going to smash your insides up. Chase after fake dreams, when all the time, right in front of you . . . why can't you see what's in front of your eyes?' And then he stormed away.

'Matt . . .' she called after him.

'No, I've had enough,' he screamed back at her. 'I've finished with you. Don't follow me.' And suddenly he was running as fast as he could.

'Matt, please,' she cried.

But he was already out of sight.

His last words echoed all through the night for Tara: 'I've finished with you.'

Next morning Tara was waiting for him at the school gate. He was very apologetic and they exchanged false, dead smiles. But something had gone from their relationship. They both knew it.

First thing on Sunday Katie was on the telephone: 'Have you heard the news?'

'What?' Tara braved herself, sensing by Katie's tone that it was not good news.

'Matt's going out with that awful Annette.'

'Since when?'

'Since last night.'

'It won't last,' said Tara at once.

'But even so, we should have stopped it.' Katie said 'we' but really she'd meant 'you'. There was no mistaking the note of rebuke in her voice.

But Matt would come back to them. This was just a temporary blip.

Tara wasn't sure if she should pray for Matt to break up with Annette. If seemed rather a negative prayer. But Tara figured Annette couldn't possibly bring Matt any happiness. After that she prayed for Rayner to be saved. Her prayers always ended with that request. She knew it would happen. She just wondered how much longer it would take . . . days . . . weeks . . . months?

It didn't matter. She lived by faith, not by sight now.

She could wait.

PART TWO

12 Six months later

It was swelteringly hot. After a cold damp April, May had begun with a heatwave.

Tara stopped on her way home to sniff some apple blossom. Spring was at its very heart now. Warm, intoxicating scents floated up from everywhere. The air was heavy today. Maybe this was why she had a faint, but distinct feeling of unease.

Oh, hurry back, Paul.

He was away on a course and wouldn't be home until six o'clock.

The house always felt so empty when he wasn't there. Easter had been agony: two very long weeks without him.

And since Easter he'd been working so hard she'd hardly seen him. Tonight she was going to tell him to relax a bit more. She was becoming worried about him; no one could keep up that pace of work for so long.

It hadn't always been like that. Every Tuesday, after the Christian Union meeting, she and Paul would go off and have a relaxing cuppa somewhere – though never at those tea rooms again. They would talk about everything. All week she'd look forward to it. And then Paul had started going with her to the Bible study class on Thursday nights; they worked all through Mark's Gospel together.

By then she'd told her grandparents that it was her not Katie who was interested in Christianity. They hadn't said much in reply, just looked warily at each other.

They did express surprise when, for her fifteenth birthday treat in March, she'd requested a day with Paul at a massive Christian get-together just outside Coventry. Tara had never seen or felt anything like it; over ten thousand people were there. Paul said it was a bit like being in heaven, mixing with so many believers, all spirit-filled.

On the way home they were both starving, so they stopped off at a very imposing restaurant. It was deserted apart from them, and Paul kept making up silly reasons why. He'd really made her laugh that night.

As they were leaving Paul had helped her on with her coat and suddenly put his arm round her. 'You're very special,' he'd whispered.

'So are you,' she'd replied. He'd held her so tightly she buried her face in the warm feel of his body. She never wanted to pull away from him.

Afterwards, neither of them mentioned what had happened. But Tara knew she'd hold that moment close to her, forever. It was just a shame she couldn't tell anyone how she felt about Paul – not even Katie or Matt. Especially not Matt. He'd just raise his eyes and give a knowing smirk as if to say, I knew you fancied him.

But this wasn't some silly schoolgirl crush. She and Paul didn't exchange furtive kisses in the kitchen. They never even held hands. It wasn't that sort of relationship. Knowing Paul was there was enough to send her spirits soaring like a kite in a high wind.

That was all she needed.

She reached her house. Grandad was outside working in the front garden. It was tiny, yet lovingly tended; a riot of late spring flowers.

'Hi, Grandad.'

He started with surprise. 'You're back early.'

'Well, I was going round to Katie's but she's got a headache. She gets them when it's very sunny.'

'I'm sorry to hear that,' he hesitated, then walked over to her. 'I think a brew is called for.' He put an arm round her as they walked into the house. 'So, how's young Tara today?' he asked, beaming at her.

'I'm fine. Is everything OK?'

'Of course it is. Your nan should be back soon. You know she's got a stall at this bring-and-buy sale?'

'Yeah, she's raised quite a lot of money for charity, hasn't she?'

'Has to keep busy, your nan,' said Grandad, who always spoke far more warmly about Nan when she wasn't there. He filled up the kettle. Then he smiled at Tara again. He was almost being too nice to her. That feeling of unease which Tara had felt all day started to grow.

Grandad put some biscuits on a plate, then said, 'Your father rang earlier.'

'Oh yeah.'

'He seems to be making a go of this job, I'll say that. Anyway, he wanted to know if you'd like to go to the theatre with him.'

'Reckon I would,' said Tara at once.

'He says he'll take you to any show you want.'

'He's amazing, isn't he?' declared Tara. 'Every so often he thinks, I'm bored today, what shall I do? I know, I'll play Tara's dad for a few hours.' She shook her head. 'He doesn't know the first thing about being a father. A proper father.' She chanted words she'd said so often before.

Grandad didn't reply at first. He stared out of the kitchen window. 'But I probably haven't been the ideal father to him,' he said.

'That's not true,' she exclaimed at once.

'Tara, I don't think you were there.' He turned round and smiled dimly at her. 'Trouble was, he never had any of the same interests as me. He never once came on any of my steam train trips or . . . When he and your nan were together I always felt cut out. And so . . . I think I short-changed him.'

'So now he short-changes me,' murmured Tara. But even as she said this an image of her dad floated into her head: he was walking away from her and, somehow, without quite knowing why, she wanted to call him back.

Only he was too far away.

She knew he'd never hear her.

Her grandad went on, 'By the way, I've got something for you, something you're not going to like.'

'What is it?'

'Priestley High is having an open day; they want the three of us to go along.' He handed her the invitation, but Tara didn't even look at it.

'No,' she said firmly. She sat down at the kitchen table. Grandad sat down heavily opposite her.

'Grandad, Rayner is going to stay open.'

'Not a hope, my young Tara,' he replied, not unkindly.

'But what about all the publicity?'

'I know you've all worked very hard ...' he shook his head regretfully.

'But we've been praying every day. I know Rayner will be saved.'

'Believe that if you like; got to believe facts, too.' Then he got up and put two tea bags into the pot. 'Of course, there are those who say the land Rayner is on was sold before you started praying.'

'I don't know why everyone's giving up!' cried Tara. Only last week at school she'd had to fill in a form saying which school she wanted to attend in September. She'd just written, Rayner, Rayner, Rayner, all over it.

'You've only got to do one year there,' said Grandad, sitting down again and placing the tray of biscuits in front of her. 'It won't be so bad.'

'But I know Rayner isn't going to close,' cried Tara. 'With God all things are possible.' She was quoting one of Paul's favourite phrases now. 'You either trust God or you don't, there's no middle way.'

Grandad sighed but didn't mention the subject again. Later when Nan came in Tara heard them both whispering together in the kitchen. Yet she was feeling relieved now; all day she'd had this horrible feeling. It was good to know the bad thing was just this encounter with Grandad about Rayner School.

There was still an hour before Paul's return. She decided the time would go more quickly if she did some homework. It was weird, really; some teachers at her school seemed to have given up and hardly set any homework, while others were trying to cram the whole GCSE syllabus into one year. So she had mountains of work to do for history, for instance. She managed to write two pages of her history essay before she heard a key turn in the lock . . .

Tara glanced at herself in the mirror, quickly doing her hair – it still didn't look right – but she couldn't wait any longer.

She half ran down the stairs. Paul, Nan and Grandad were all in Paul's room, all standing up. They looked strangely uncertain, like actors who hadn't quite mastered their roles. Paul smiled at her but it was such a faraway smile it was rather frightening. She noticed Paul had a bottle of wine in his hand. Following her gaze, Nan said, in an oddly formal voice, 'The wine is from us . . . Paul has some good news, but sad news for us. He's got a new job in Leicester, starting in

September. So it's wonderful that he's secured his future, but obviously we're sorry that Paul is leaving.'

In a kind of daze Tara said, 'So you didn't go on a course then?'

'No, I didn't,' replied Paul sharply.

Tara didn't recognise the voice as his. She gazed rather wildly around the room. Sometimes in dreams – bad dreams – Tara would hear a voice whisper, 'Don't worry, this isn't real, you're only dreaming.' Tara could hear that voice now. For this didn't feel right at all; it wasn't really happening.

And Nan wasn't really saying to her, 'Jobs are difficult to come by and Paul's got to make his own way, think about his future. He went to this interview with the headmaster's blessing. He's done very well today.'

Was Tara supposed to answer? She couldn't.

'You'd better keep in touch now, Paul,' said Grandad.

'Oh, I will.'

'And perhaps we can pop up and see you – when you've got settled in, of course.' Grandad smiled.

'That would be splendid,' said Paul. 'You've been just brilliant to me, made me feel right at home. I'll miss you all.' For the first time since he'd got back he looked directly at Tara. She immediately turned away.

'Why don't I show you what I got up to in the garden while you were away,' murmured Grandad to Nan who took the hint.

'We won't be long,' she said.

Nan and Grandad were letting Paul explain in private why he was leaving Rayner, leaving her.

Paul stared across at her. Suddenly they seemed a long way from each other. 'I don't want to go . . .' he began.

'So why go?'

'It is for the best,' he half-chanted.

'For the best,' she repeated incredulously. 'You mean, you've secured your future?'

'If you like, yes.'

'But Rayner isn't going to close. We've asked God to save our school. And God likes to answer prayer. You're always saying that.'

Paul seldom looked unsure, but he did then. 'Yes, all right. Look we're not bigger than God; he's got the overall plan.'

'So what are you saying?'

'God's will is always right, so maybe the closure of Rayner will bring many more blessings than if the school stays open.'

'That's not true.'

'From your point of view, maybe, but . . . sometimes I've prayed for something and it doesn't happen.'

'So it's just luck then.'

'No, no.'

'And what about the voice I heard saying Rayner lives? What was that?'

'OK, let me think about it, all right?' There was an edge of irritation in his voice which Tara had never heard before. 'Maybe that message . . .' he faltered.

'Don't worry about it,' snapped Tara. 'Just don't worry. Still, it's funny really, isn't it, you go round asking us to pray for Rayner, telling us to have faith, it's not going to close . . .' her voice caught suddenly in her throat.

'I didn't say that,' his voice was very low.

'Oh yes you did,' she cried accusingly. 'You said after we've prayed we'd see doors opening up everywhere, you said with God anything is possible, and we believed you. Meanwhile, what do you do – you sneak off and get another job. It's funny really, it's . . .'

'Tara, stop it, listen to me! I prayed and prayed about what to do.' His voice was anguished, but he couldn't meet her eyes.

'Oh, did you really?' she replied scornfully. 'Still, your religion's quite useful, isn't it? When you want to chuck your girlfriend you say it's because she's not a Christian . . .'

There was no smile on his face now. She'd hit a nerve. She should have stopped there, but she wanted to go on wounding, wounding. 'And now you're bored with the Rayner campaign – and me – so you just say a few prayers, and escape that too. Actually, I think you're afraid to commit to people, that's why . . . Matt was right, none of it's been real has it? Not my faith, not you. Especially not you.'

And then she was out of the door in a flash. She ran, almost without realising it, towards Hart Lane. In the past she'd often gone there to think and pray. And she always felt healed afterwards. But tonight it had turned into a dark, sinister place, thick with stinging nettles and shadows. This was what it had always been, of course. Another illusion. Her life was full of them. She tried to cry. But she couldn't. She couldn't feel anything. She was lost in the tangle of her own thoughts.

Crashing through everything she saw Paul's face the moment after she'd told him her faith wasn't real, and neither was he. Those words must have come at him like a fireball, leaving him devastated. His face just seemed to crumple. She'd never seen him so affected before. And *she*'d done it. She'd really gone for the jugular. That was a nasty, vicious thing she'd said to him.

And now some tears did escape. She couldn't cry for herself but she could cry for Paul, for what she'd done to him. She cried in shuddering bursts, tears of pain and defeat and emptiness.

How could she give so much pain to someone she loved? She knew she was wounding him, yet she went on stabbing, stabbing, stabbing. But Paul was abandoning her, a voice shrieked inside her. Or was he? Could Paul, the person she'd spent so many hours with, just abandon her? Well, Phil did. But Paul was totally different. She said Paul's name again, letting the familiar glow his name aroused steal over her.

He can't really want to leave her. These last months had meant so much to her; they must have meant something to him too.

She'd persuade him to stay, after she'd apologised to him from the bottom of her heart. Everything could still be sorted out.

She hurried home. Nan was waiting for her in the doorway. 'We really can't have this,' she said crossly, 'just running out of the house without a word to anyone. We've all been worried sick. We rang up Katie and Matt and they didn't know where you were. It won't do.'

Tara looked at her watch. She'd been gone much longer than she'd thought.

'I'm sorry, Nan,' she whispered. 'Where's Paul?'

Nan's face softened. 'He's gone, love.'

'Gone,' echoed Tara disbelievingly.

'Yes, he's gone to stay at a friend's tonight, he thought it would be for the best, until you've had a chance to . . . Tara, if your school closes Paul would be without a job, so you can't expect him . . .'

'No,' interrupted Tara tonelessly, 'I can't.'

So Paul couldn't face her. He'd enlisted Nan to act as his spokesperson. Well, Nan was an improvement on the weasel-faced guy Phil had used.

Paul was walking away from her and he wasn't looking back. But he needn't worry. She wouldn't pester him any more. Once people have closed the door on you, it never opens again. She knew that. Only, she was locking the door on him too.

'It's OK, Nan, I'm fine, just a bit tired,' she even managed a slight smile. 'I'm going to bed now.'

'All right, love,' said Nan. 'I'll bring you up a hot drink and a snack; there's no point in going to bed hungry as you won't sleep.'

Tara doubted if she'd sleep a wink tonight but she didn't say anything. She started going up the stairs, then she turned round. 'By the way, Nan, he won't be coming back, you know.'

13 'Such a sad day'

The school hall was packed; it hadn't been this full since the Rescue Rayner meeting last September. It was the same mix as before: current pupils, ex-pupils, parents. Tara waved to Nan and Grandad who arrived with Katie's mum. This time, though, there was much more mingling; everyone spoke to everyone else: everyone belonged.

The headmaster appeared, making his typical slow, thoughtful way to the stage. And, as usual, there was silence. But today he twisted his face into a kind of smile. 'It's good of you to be here to join in our final assembly.'

This really was it, thought Tara. This Friday afternoon wasn't just the last day of term, it was Rayner's last breath. Yet it was hard to take in, perhaps because these final days had been so topsy-turvy and – it must be admitted – exciting.

The whole school had gone to Alton Towers, hired a cinema for the afternoon, and put on a review. The school football team had scored an amazing victory, perhaps because the school had things to prove, but also, as someone commented, 'They were able to pass that ball without looking up; they seemed, somehow, to read each other's mind.' And there can't have been many teams who were cheered on by every single member of their school.

In the last days of Rayner there was a feeling of exclusivity and triumph even while the computer equipment was being dismantled and tables and chairs were fast disappearing. Names were scrawled enthusiastically on just about every remaining table.

Today people had raced around the school signing shirts and taking photographs. The spate of water fights, which had been building up over the past couple of weeks, reached its climax in a huge battle at lunch-time. Even a couple of teachers joined in.

Now the headmaster was handing out the prizes for special achievement. There were far more prizes this year. Tara, for the first time, gained one for English, Katie for French. Then came the sports prizes, culminating in the football trophy. To a great roar of applause the football team filed out and then insisted that Paul, who'd trained them after school, take a bow as well. So Paul, somewhat shyly, joined them, to further tumultuous applause.

Tara's face stiffened. Ever since Paul had moved out she'd barely spoken to him. As she'd suspected, he never moved back. He did try to talk to her several times, yet each time she'd fled. She had no alternative. For she'd driven the pain she felt about Paul deep inside her. And that was where it must remain.

She'd also stopped going to Paul's Christian Union meetings. One day a couple of the girls from the group came up and said how much they missed her. They sounded quite genuine, although Tara wondered if Paul had put them up to it. She told them she couldn't pray any more but she was still reading the Bible every night. And that was true. She'd reached St Paul's letter to the Corinthians now. Last night she'd read over and over the words: 'There is nothing love cannot face; there is no limit to its faith, its hope and its endurance. Love will never come to an end.'

Such wonderful words. They called up something in Tara. It was just a shame they weren't true. Of course love came to an end. People died, for goodness sake. And you were left with your insides torn out.

Months after her mum died she remembered hearing her dad cry. She thought he would never stop. It was a terrible sound. And she didn't so much feel sorry for him, as scared.

People died. Just as Rayner was about to die. Despite all the prayers, God was not going to do anything.

'Rayner lives.' That voice can't have been from God. It was just a fragment of a dream, perhaps, or wanting to hear something so much you conjure it up. Whatever the explanation, it wasn't real. And maybe her vision wasn't either.

There were more loud cheers for Paul as each member of the staff was briefly celebrated, followed by the caretaker and all the dinner ladies. And then came the video of the school's last week: quirky, funny interviews with pupils, staff and governors; shots of the school at Alton Towers and that famous football win; infamous shots of Matt doing his *Dirty Dancing* impersonation at the school review (in everyone's opinion, the highlight); and the finale – a group shot of the entire school.

When the video was switched off there was silence for a moment. The headmaster gazed around the hall and said, 'They tell me this is the end of Rayner School. In a few weeks' time they will start building sixty houses here; Rayner will be gone, forgotten.' His voice was suddenly little more than a hoarse whisper. 'But I believe nothing good ever really dies; I believe Rayner will live on for a long time yet.'

Then he got down off the stage and began shaking hands with everyone who was there. People stood up somewhat awkwardly at first while the headmaster greeted each of them by name.

Tara watched as he made his way down her row; nobody actually bowed to him although a few came close. Then he was shaking Katie's hand. 'Delighted with your progress, especially in French. Best of luck, Katie.'

'Thank you,' gasped Katie so reverently that Tara had to smother a smile.

Next he was shaking Tara's hand. 'Some very encouraging results. Congratulations on your English prize. Good luck in the future.'

Tara was certain her voice sounded as awed as Katie's. Not entirely surprising – it was as if this regal figure had suddenly descended from Mount Olympus.

Matt, who was standing next to Tara, grinned at the headmaster. 'I'm afraid I haven't won any prizes.'

The headmaster gave a hint of a smile. 'Keep up the dancing, Matthew. Best of luck in the future.'

Afterwards Matt started shaking his hand in the air. 'What a grip that guy's got.'

After each person's hand had been shaken, the headmaster made his slow, impassive way to the stage again. Only, now, everyone had got to their feet. Applause rained on him from every corner. He was like a captain going down with his ship. He was leaving education today; taking early retirement. This was the end for him too.

The applause raged on until, finally, he raised his hand. 'That ends our assembly.' Then that grave face relaxed into a smile. 'But I believe there is a party in the drama theatre. All, of course, are welcome. So, as I think they say, party on.'

Ordinarily, a headmaster using a vaguely hip phrase would have been frowned upon. But today it was just one more acknowledgement that the barriers were down; everyone was in this together. People slowly got up, a few were unashamedly weeping. Katie looked pale and tight-lipped. Tara gave her a hug.

'Well, let's do what the man said,' said Matt briskly, 'and party on.' So, after Tara had said goodbye to her grandparents, she and Katie followed him into the drama theatre.

The party began with a great burst of noise and energy. There was a lot of mad dancing, not to mention a brief encore of the water fight. But then everything seemed to sag dramatically. There were more tears. Tara even found herself hugging Olivia Jackson who was becoming quite hysterical. And then people left quite speedily. Teachers were going round shaking hands now.

And suddenly Paul was shaking Tara's hand. 'Goodbye Tara. Lots of luck.'

'Thanks,' she replied, shakily.

All of a sudden he was staring at her, 'Tara . . .' he began, but he was pulled away from her by one of the football team.

And then he was gone.

For one mad moment she wanted to run after him, finish their conversation, say goodbye properly. But then, she thought wearily, what was the point? What could she say to him? They were a million miles from each other now. Anyway, if he'd really wanted to speak to her he'd have found her again.

'Would you like to come back to my place?' asked Katie. 'Matt's coming too.'

'Best offer you'll get tonight,' said Matt.

The three of them left arm in arm. Normally when Matt finished school he would be rushing off to Annette's, or on the days she had games and ended school early, she'd be waiting by the gate. But even Annette seemed to have recognised that tonight was sacred, so it was just the three of them again, reeling all the way to Katie's as if they were very drunk, and then laughing, until Tara had a pain, at some ancient snaps of them which Katie had found.

145

For weeks she and Matt had been freezingly polite to each other. But tonight it was as if they'd slipped back to an easier, happier time, and soon they were making silly cracks about each other again.

'We're family,' declared Matt. 'And we always will be.'

Tara arrived home much later than she had planned. 'Sorry I'm late, Nan, but I went round Katie's and . . .'

'That's all right, dear.' Nan was sitting in what Tara still thought of as Paul's room. 'Such a sad day, isn't it?' Tara's throat tightened. 'But at least the old school went out in style, didn't it? That's something.'

'Yes,' murmured Tara. She fell into the chair opposite Nan. 'Grandad out?'

'Should be back any minute. Now, have you eaten?'

'Oh yeah, I couldn't eat another thing . . .' she looked across at Nan. 'What are you making now?'

'I'm making some cushion covers for the raffle at the hospital.'

'You're always busy doing something, aren't you?' began Tara. She was on the edge of tears. She took a breath. 'Nan, can I ask you something?'

'Of course.' Nan put down her sewing.

'You know you said you used to be religious, do you still believe in God?'

Nan shifted uneasily. 'Well . . . I'm not a regular churchgoer any more but I like to go at Christmas . . . and, yes, I do believe.' She looked at Tara questioningly.

'It's just I not only believed in God, I thought I had this hotline to him. I thought he sent me messages, like "Rayner lives".' The words

146

repeated themselves mockingly in her head, 'Rayner lives. Rayner lives.' Her voice rose over them. 'In the Bible it says, "He could do no mighty deeds because of their unbelief," but I believed, Nan. Each night I prayed for Rayner and I really thought it was going to be saved.' She gave a harsh laugh. 'But I was wrong. I was just fooling myself. And as for God . . .'

There was silence for a moment, then Nan said, quietly, 'Just because we want something to happen and it doesn't – well, that doesn't mean there isn't a God.'

'No, maybe. I don't know.' Tara shrugged her shoulders and stood up. She noticed a large box of chocolates on the table.

'Who are the chocs from?'

'Paul.'

'Paul's been here?' The words seemed to scratch at her heart.

'Oh, yes, he came round to say goodbye. Said he wanted to speak to you; hung on for ages.'

Tara gazed around at the aching emptiness of his room. Suddenly a loud sob burst from her. It surprised Nan – and her. Now tears were streaming down her face. She couldn't hold them back.

Nan got up and rocked Tara gently in her arms. And, still sobbing, Tara was struck by a memory: she was a little girl, no more than seven, running home crying because they'd been making comments at school about her not having a mum and dad. And she'd run straight into Nan's arms. Nan would make it better by listening and comforting – and at just the right moment produce a large packet of sweets. Now she made 'a nice cup of tea'.

As Tara sat drinking it she said fiercely, 'I wasn't crying because of Paul, you know.'

'No, of course not,' replied Nan, soothingly.

'I was just crying because . . .' then she stared across at Nan. 'You knew I cared about him, didn't you?'

'Yes I did,' said Nan gently.

'I suppose you think I've been very silly.'

'Paul's a nice lad, a gentleman. Besides caring about someone is never silly. In the end, caring about people is the only thing which makes any sense.'

'Do you think so?'

'Oh yes. Being needed by someone . . . that's what's made me happy and content these last forty years. First there was your father – he was such a frail baby, you know. They didn't think he'd last the night. So it was like a miracle when he did. And he still needed constant care and attention to make sure he was thriving and developing. But I loved it all, just as I've loved looking after you.'

Tara grinned. 'I bet.'

'And as for your grandad . . . why, I've had to look after him ever since he came out of the army forty years ago.'

Tara couldn't help a slightly sceptical look coming on to her face.

Nan went on. 'Oh I know your grandad would never admit it of course, but he needs me all right. Do you remember the time I had flu?'

'Yes I do. The house was a shambles and Grandad became quite demented.'

'He went to pieces,' corrected Nan proudly. 'That man wouldn't last five minutes without me sorting him out, nagging him, putting up with his funny ways . . .' she shook her head. 'I don't think God's just in a church, you know. Surely he's in the people we care about; the ones who make us forget ourselves.' She got up. 'More tea?'

'Thanks, Nan.'

Tara stared into the distance. Despite everything, she wished with all her heart she'd said goodbye to Paul.

14 Letter to Paul

17 Camber Road

October 29th

Dear Paul

I expect you are very surprised to be getting a letter from me.
In my head I have written to you so many times; but now I've
got to rush this letter because . . .

I'll explain why, in a moment, but first, how are you? We
loved your postcards and letter, which made us all laugh out

150

loud, but none of them told us much about you. So I really hope all is going well and you're not missing us too much. Ha-ha.

As for me, well let's say life is getting better. Definite low point was starting at Priestley High. It seemed so cold and impersonal. Of course, all the Rayner pupils hung around together. There was no mixing between the two schools at all, apart from a few fights. Two teachers from Rayner are at Priestley, by the way: Mr Howard and Miss Edwards, the librarian. She's been really good. Most days I go into the library to have a chat with her. She said, 'I know it's hard and I don't like it much here either, but it will get better.' And I suppose it has. Of course, Matt was going out with a girl from Priestley High (and he still is, would you believe?), and with his easy-going personality he fits in quite easily. Katie's just started going out with this sixth former; Harry Niven. He's quite nice, actually, good fun but very well-mannered – Katie said he reminds her a bit of you. I think she is well smitten. I'm really happy for her.

Katie's disappointed with her French, though. After all her success last year, she's asked to go down a set. But then I don't think anyone from Rayner is doing as well as they did last year. Another thing, you know the council said we'd get free bus passes? Well now they've changed it so that only the fifth years will get free passes. Everyone else has to pay. Lots of hassle here over that. Talk about sneaky.

By the way, it's about time I apologised to you. Back in May

I said some terrible things to you. I won't remind you of what they were; I hope you'll have forgotten them. (Please forget them!) You are a totally free agent, free to move to Leicester or anywhere else you choose. I don't own you, I know. SORRY. SORRY. SORRY. (Note the emphasis.) It's just I was so convinced that Rayner would stay open. I had faith. And when it didn't, well, to be honest, I became quite confused about that.

I'll tell you who's been quite helpful to me though – amazingly – Olivia Jackson. She's also interested in Christianity and we've had some long chats (she says hello, by the way). Then, a couple of weeks ago, we went to hear John Morley again in a church hall (so there was no Bingo before we went in!). Afterwards we chatted to him for quite a long while – told him all about Rayner closing – and this time he was very helpful.

He said that faith is nothing more or less than trusting God, which means we carry on believing even when we don't get what we want from him. This is true, I suppose. But it's really hard, isn't it? There are times when I still feel full of muddle and doubt. Quite a lot of times, actually.

Just as I was saying goodbye to John he said to me, 'Remember, Tara, nothing can separate us from the love of God.' I think those words must have got into my bloodstream. I can't stop thinking about them. I think about my vision a lot, too. I even told my dad about it. I bet that surprised you.

It was all very strange, really. For weeks he'd been pestering me to go out with him to see a show. Katie said to me, 'He's asking you out because he's feeling guilty, so why not use his guilt and go and see something, making sure he gets you the best seats?'

So that's what happened. We went to see *Phantom of the Opera* (best seats), then he took me out for a meal.

It was a terribly awkward conversation. I had a bit of a go at him, actually; told him what a terrible father he'd been. Well, it's the truth. Anyway, he took it. I'll say that for him. Then he asked me about how I'd become interested in Christianity. And that's when I told him about the vision.

He seemed amazed, especially when I told him it had taken place in Hart Lane. I don't expect he imagined teenage girls had such experiences!

He asked about you, as well. I think he's jealous. I can't blame him. Paul – I don't want to make you big-headed – but I miss you so much. You opened up a whole new way of looking at things for me. I'll always be grateful to you for that . . . and all those times we shared. Now I feel as if someone very special has vanished from my life.

Perhaps I shouldn't write like this to you. It's what I feel and yet I'm afraid to tell you. But then people often run to the hills when you open your heart to them. That's why we spend so much of our lives pretending and hiding. It frustrates me, yet I spend most of my time doing just the same.

It was like those weeks after you moved out; you tried so often to speak to me, I know, and each time I just ran away.

Just seeing you . . . well the pain was like a terrible fire inside me just eating me up. So I thought I was protecting myself. We all put barbed-wire fences round ourselves, don't we? To keep ourselves safe. And yet, behind those fences it gets so lonely.

I never even said goodbye to you – not properly. That's why . . . and now I come to the totally crazy part of my letter, and the reason I'm rushing it to you now. Would you believe, the bulldozers are moving in on Rayner School next week? The council claim it's because there's been all sorts of trouble at the school – gangs hanging around, fires starting, especially at night. Others reckon the real reason is that the land was sold some time before the school was closed!

Anyway, before the school is smashed to pieces there's going to be a kind of vigil to see it off in some style. We're all meeting outside Rayner on Thursday 2 November at 8.30pm. It would be *wonderful* if you could be there. I know it's very short notice and Leicester's about three and a half hours away in the car, so if you can't make it, I shall *totally understand*.

But if you can be there, it would make me very happy.

Nan and Grandad send their love. So do I. All of it.

Tara

XX

PS I hope you don't mind me writing. I really don't want to be a nuisance.

15 The vision

Tara approached Rayner School. She'd returned for one night only. With her were Matt, Katie and Katie's boyfriend, Harry. Just behind them were Katie's mum and little sister and Tara's nan and grandad; all with their lighted candles, Nan holding hers high in the air as if it were some kind of trophy.

Ahead of them people streamed through the school gates, while winding right the way down the road were many more supporters. Maybe it was seeing that long line of people, all with their candles, which made Tara feel she was part of some great pilgrimage. They weren't going to give up their school to the darkness; tonight it would be aglow with light once more.

A little girl bobbed up to Tara. The girl was holding her candle with great concentration, smiling companionably. Tara smiled back. Then her mother rushed up: 'Don't go running ahead now, Becky, keep with us.' She added, apologetically, 'She's rather excited, she's really too young for this but I wanted her to see it.'

Matt nudged Tara and Katie. 'Picture this: some poor old geek and his missus think, we'll retire to Rayner; nice quiet little village, nothing ever happens there. And then the first night they're here, they crack open the twiglets, then they decide to go for a little drive around their village. Only, when they pass this venerable school, Mr Geek almost crashes the car, because – well look at it! They probably think we all belong to some weird cult which sacrifices geeks every Thursday night.'

'Your turn tonight, is it?' quipped Tara.

'Ha, ha,' said Matt.

'But actually, this could be the beginning of a horror story, couldn't it?' said Katie. She turned excitedly to her boyfriend, who was holding a torch, which Tara thought was cheating.

'I just think it's wonderful so many people have turned up,' said Katie's mum, behind her.

'Oh, it's wonderful, all right,' agreed Katie. 'But it's eerie, too.'

They joined the blaze of candles illuminating the school. People thronged into the school grounds shouting out greetings to half-remembered faces.

Honoured guests were a knot of old people from the flats at the other end of the village, who remembered the very first days of Rayner. They stood in their scarves and big overcoats, gently stamping their feet to keep warm.

'This is turning into the mother and grandmother of all reunions,' Matt observed. Just about everyone was here except . . .

Tara became angry with herself. She really mustn't expect Paul to turn up tonight . . . then she wouldn't be disappointed. After all, it was pretty unlikely he'd drive all this way just to come to some kind of wake for a school he'd left four months ago. Paul will have moved on in his life now, made lots of new friends. Probably the very last thing he wanted was a letter from some drippy fifteen-year-old from days gone by.

He'll have thrown the letter away by now, of course.

'Ow,' she cried suddenly, then flushed. 'It's all right, a bit of candle wax just burnt my hand.'

'Someone call an ambulance,' grinned Matt.

'Hold your candle a little higher, Tara, dear,' said Nan. 'I used to take a candle up to bed every night when I was younger, you know.'

'Nan, that makes you sound about a hundred.'

'That'd be right,' chuckled Grandad. 'She's years older than me, you know.'

'What nonsense,' replied Nan, crisply. 'I know exactly how old you are and if you keep on like that I'll tell them all . . . No, I lived on a farm when I was younger and there was no electricity but we didn't miss it. We didn't have any television or videos or computer games or . . .'

'But you made your own entertainment, didn't you?' broke in Tara, smiling.

'That's right,' said Nan.

'And in those days you could buy a car and a house and twenty gobstoppers and still have change out of a five-pound note, couldn't you?' said Matt.

Nan smiled, half amused. Then, handing her candle to Grandad, started foraging about in the bag she'd brought with her. She produced two flasks and a sandwich box. 'Tea, coffee, anyone?' Tara shifted uncomfortably. She wasn't sure she approved of Nan turning tonight into a picnic.

'Ladies and gentlemen,' called a voice. Tara dimly recognised the man speaking through a megaphone as someone who'd been in the sixth form the year she started at Rayner. 'It's wonderful to see so many of you here tonight to honour Rayner, our school.'

There were ripples of agreement which grew louder as he outlined the special role Rayner had played in the community. Tara couldn't help reflecting that a number of people agreeing so vocally with him had never actually sent their children to Rayner – and others had taken them away as soon as the school was in trouble. If they'd shown a little more faith, Rayner might still be open.

A hush fell as the headmaster was introduced. The light from his candle seemed to hollow out his face, emptying it of any energy or vitality. He looked years older than he had in the summer, now he seemed to be fading back into the past, already a ghost. He didn't speak this time, either, just bowed slowly.

And then a small choir began singing 'Jerusalem'. Tara could remember hearing this hymn on television at the *Last Night of the Proms*, accompanied by massed cheering and waving of flags; then it had just seemed like one more jolly sing-along. Now with only four voices filling the air it became brave and defiant.

There was a reprise of 'Jerusalem' with everyone urged to join in. Around Tara rose Nan's high, rather pleasing voice and Grandad's heavy croak, and Katie singing very faintly but standing so close to Tara she could smell the shampoo in her hair. For some reason, everyone seemed to be drawing in closer. Matt gave Tara a nudge: 'They'll have us singing carols next,' he said.

Tara laughed. And then she heard her name explode out of the darkness.

She turned round and cried, 'Paul!' so loudly, everyone around her stopped singing. And then Nan was exclaiming too, while Paul sauntered up to them in such an easy, relaxed way, it was as if time was playing another of its tricks tonight, and he'd never gone away at all, and had just wandered down the road from Tara's house.

'But Paul . . . How did you know about this?' spluttered Nan.

'Tara dropped me a line.' He said this very lightly, but Tara still found herself blushing.

'I thought Paul would like to know about this,' she said.

'And isn't it brilliant?' declared Paul. 'It feels as if half the village is here.'

'Now, have you eaten?' demanded Nan.

'I had a snack before I came out . . .' began Paul.

'That must have been hours ago,' said Nan. 'Now, we've got tea and coffee – and we've still got some sandwiches all wrapped in foil, so they're nice and fresh. We've got . . .'

'Let the lad catch his breath,' interrupted Grandad.

But Nan was in full flight now. 'If I'd known you were coming . . .' a pointed stare at Tara now, '. . . I'd have brought much more food with me.'

While Nan fussed around Paul, Tara could only gaze at him in a kind of wonderment. He was really here. And it was her letter which had conjured him up. Her letter! Wasn't life just utterly wonderful sometimes?

'What are you smiling about?' murmured Katie. 'Or shall I just guess?'

After Paul had wolfed down a couple of sandwiches, Tara handed him her candle.

'But what about you?' he asked.

'That's OK, I think you deserve it,' she said. Her hand wouldn't stop trembling anyway.

'We'll share it, then,' he whispered.

Meanwhile the singing had stopped and now a man was recalling the first day of Rayner School over seventy years ago. He wore a large woollen scarf round his head and his voice was high and quavery. Yet he described teachers – who later lost their lives in the Second World War – with such skill and affection that Tara could picture them. It was as if they were magically released into the cold night once more.

Then finally came three, full-throated cheers for the school. The

160

noise was tremendous and seemed to go on and on. A glorious explosion of sound. And afterwards a tremendous rush of exhilaration; a feeling that something had been achieved tonight.

'I'm going to give Harry the fifty pence tour of the school,' announced Katie. 'Are you coming?' She looked at Tara and Paul, who both nodded.

As they walked inside the school two policemen hovered self-consciously. 'Watch your candles in there,' one of them called.

'Can't let anything happen to the school before the bulldozers arrive tomorrow, can we?' said Katie bitterly.

Very soon Tara was wishing they hadn't returned. She didn't know what she was expecting: that the school would somehow be magically preserved like the *Marie Celeste*, with everything exactly as they'd left it? Of course it wasn't anything like that. It was just a shadowy relic now. 'It's dead already,' whispered Tara as the four of them stood in Katie's and her old form room, her words lingering around the bare walls. Katie and Harry were already retreating outside. Tara made as if to follow them, then hesitated. So did Paul. She'd been waiting anxiously for a moment alone with him. Now she felt oddly shy. Paul stood smiling at her, his candle lighting up her face.

'I'm really glad you told me about this,' he said.

'Are you?' Tara's voice sounded more questioning than she'd intended. 'So how are you?'

'Not so bad.' From anyone else that would be an everyday comment; but from Paul that was surprisingly negative. She wasn't quite sure how to respond.

'Everyone misses you,' she said suddenly.

'I miss them,' said Paul, staring right at her.

'The last day of term Nan said you came round to the house – and you waited for me. Was there . . . was it about anything in particular? Or maybe you don't remember,' she laughed nervously.

'Hey, I remember all right,' said Paul. He sighed deeply, then shook his head. 'Look, really I came round for myself. I didn't want you to think I left because I didn't care. The truth was, I cared too much.' He rushed on, speaking all in a gabble. 'I knew I had to go. I realised it at Easter. After Easter I spoke to your grandparents. They were really good. They understood I didn't want to do anything to harm you. They knew things were getting out of control. It seemed the best way. I had to go.'

At once Tara remembered something Nan had said about Paul: 'He's a gentleman.' Yes, there was something very gallant about what Paul had done. She was flattered and moved and yet, she felt cheated, too. Paul discovers he cares about Tara, so immediately he falls upon his sword and ends everything, robbing her of so much.

'I wish you'd told me before,' began Tara.

'I know, it was just . . . very difficult. I felt I had no right to tell you really, it would just have made things harder for you – I was in agony there, Tara,' he cried suddenly.

'I know, but Paul, I wish . . . I wish,' but it was impossible to put into words what she wished. Instead, she stared bleakly around her. 'I wish Rayner hadn't lost.'

'So do I.' He said this so forcefully, Tara gazed at him in surprise.

'Almost up to the end I thought the school was going to stay open, you know. And that night when you were demanding answers from me about it – well, you saw through me all right, didn't you? I didn't have any. For I thought, I thought . . .' he struggled for a moment. 'Jesus is as alive today as he was in the early days of the church – I really believe that. And I've seen so many wonderful things, miracles you wouldn't believe. So saving a school – a really good school – that seemed quite a small miracle,' he gave a rueful smile. 'I've been struggling with my faith for quite a while, you know,' his tone became confiding. 'Then last week I had a big disaster.'

'What?' asked Tara, staring intently at him.

'Well, you know I did that assembly about how I became a Christian?' Tara nodded. 'They asked me to do that talk at my new school. No problem, I thought. So there I was, taking assembly Friday morning, nearly four hundred faces staring at me, and I completely died. I just stood there speechless in front of the whole assembly,' his voice started to shake. 'In the end the deputy head had to help me off the stage . . . talk about humiliating myself.'

'What do you think happened?' Tara's heart leapt to him.

'Just couldn't do it, Tara . . . I'd lost my faith and I'd lost myself. But that night I read Psalm 27 – one of my favourite psalms: "Be strong and let your heart take courage . . . wait for the Lord," then I prayed to God, no demands, just said I needed him. And straight away I felt such peace, such love. He was there, Tara.' She nodded in agreement. 'But before, I'd been blocking him out. It's like you said in your letter, you've just got to trust God. He's the one with the master plan and one day, "My knowledge will be whole, like God's knowledge of me." ' He paused, then smiled at Tara.

'I'll tell you something else, the following morning your letter arrived. And Tara, when you invited me here, I really believe God was working through you. For what I've seen and I don't mean this . . .' he gestured at the classroom, '. . . that's just the shell. No, out there, all those people; that wonderful spirit. Rayner lives, all right . . . Thank you for summoning me up tonight.'

She smiled up at him, 'You make me sound like a magician.'

'Perhaps you are.' His eyes were fixed on her now.

'Paul, I didn't know you were here,' called a voice. There was no more time to talk. In fact, Tara hardly saw Paul after that; they were both swallowed up in a sea of faces and flashbulbs as everyone bunched together in massive groups, as if they were all guests at some nocturnal wedding.

The wind started up, blowing out some of the candles and taking with it some of the evening's mood of mysterious enchantment. People started to leave, pilgrims no longer, just a dark swarm now.

Matt rushed over to Tara. 'If you want to play your big farewell scene, now's the time, Paul's off.'

She ran. Paul was waiting by the school entrance, half-leaning against his car. Nan and Grandad were with him.

'Hurry up,' called Nan, 'Paul's got a four-hour journey ahead of him.' Then she and Grandad edged tactfully away.

Paul smiled shyly at her. 'Take good care of yourself.'

Her eyes were smarting. She could hardly look at him. 'And you.'

'May I write?'

'You'd better.'

He grinned, then touched her arm. 'Rayner lives.' He whispered this so tenderly the words became a gift.

And then he drove round a corner and became invisible again.

She stood there aching with love and longing and tenderness. She felt as if she was saying goodbye to him forever. No, that couldn't be true. She would see him again. She would.

'Fancy Paul driving all that way tonight.' Tara whirled round to see Matt grinning at her. 'That was almost impressive.'

'And that sounds almost like a compliment.'

'Dig a bit harder and it might turn into one. Anyway, this is for you.' He handed her a brick: 'Genuine Rayner.'

'Oh, thank you, Matt.'

'Something to show your grandchildren. I'm sure they'll be fascinated . . . never know, one day they might want to put our bricks in a museum.'

'And us with them, probably.'

'Probably,' he took the brick from under her arm, put it down then hugged her tightly.

'You're so special, Matt,' she whispered.

He immediately laughed and let her go.

Tara was gasping slightly, 'Well, it's a good thing Annette's not here,' she teased.

'It's all right, I told her you've got this massive crush on me, but as I'm not interested in you, it's all perfectly safe . . . Anyway, I can't stand around here chatting I've got some bricks to deliver. I wanted you to have the first one. You'd better look after it.'

'I'll water it every day,' smiled Tara.

Tara's grandparents were ready to leave now and so was Tara. But when they got home Tara knew she couldn't go in just yet. Her head was racing. 'Look, I'm just going to get a breath of fresh air.'

'What now?' exclaimed Nan.

'I'll sleep better if I do, Nan. But I'll only be five minutes. I promise.'

'Well, don't go far.'

'I won't,' cried Tara. She was already down the road when she heard her nan calling something else after her. She couldn't make out what it was but she just called back: 'Five minutes, I promise.'

Almost instinctively she was making for Hart Lane. The wind was picking up now, swirling dead leaves into the air. The trees stirred and creaked mysteriously.

A whole year had passed now since Tara saw . . . what was it? Her imagination playing tricks? Some kind of hallucination? No, Tara was certain that white light had come from outside herself. Just when she had been at the bottom of her resources she had made a connection with something so powerful and so loving . . .

Maybe she couldn't have photographed what she saw. Maybe it wasn't real anyway. But that didn't matter. What she saw was true. And it would always be an anchor for her.

How often had she returned here, desperate to see that light again? Sometimes she'd stand for hours, eyes straining after something she'd probably never see again.

But tonight she didn't need to search for her light. It was here.

It was here in the dark smell of the earth and the leaves. It was here in the wind stirring against her hair. It was here in the trees etched against the sky.

It had been here all the time. Now at last she could see it.

'Thank you, God,' she whispered. 'And thank you for returning Paul; tonight has filled my heart – and please go on helping me.'

After that brief prayer she decided she'd better go back or Nan would start getting cranky. Then for the second time that evening she heard someone call her name. She stumbled out of Hart Lane to find her dad walking towards her. She stared at him in bewilderment.

'What are you doing here . . .?' she demanded.

'Well, I came a bit earlier, actually. I was going to attend the farewell to the school, but when I got there the place was so packed . . .' he smiled apologetically. 'I lost my bottle, I suppose.'

Tara felt a tug of sympathy for him. She remembered peering in the window at a party once and thinking she couldn't go in, there were just too many people milling about. But she didn't say anything.

'So,' he continued, 'I've been waiting at the house for you all to get back, then when your nan told me you'd gone for a walk . . . well it was you I wanted to speak to, really, to thank you.'

'Thank me?' exclaimed Tara incredulously.

'What you told me about your vision. It was just here, wasn't it?'

'That's right,' said Tara cautiously.

'Well, I've been thinking and thinking about it . . . And it has helped me,' he added nervously.

Tara was stunned.

'You know when they told me your mother had died I didn't believe them. I really thought, when she sees me she'll open her eyes. But she didn't. And that was the end of me.

'She was a very remarkable woman, your mother. And she was my guiding light. Because I was never very popular, I knew most people thought of me as a mummy's boy. But she didn't. And when I'd come home miserable, she could always bring me out of it. She saw something else in me. No one else saw it. Not even me,' he gave a dry laugh. 'So when she was gone that was the end of me.

'Your nan would say to me, "Life goes on, son," but it didn't . . . there was nothing else. Finally, I suppose you try and get by . . . but then what you told me . . .' his voice shook suddenly. 'This little life can't be all there is, can it?'

'No, I don't believe it is,' whispered Tara. She gazed up at him. For the first time, she was looking at someone she knew. 'I wish I'd told you about it before,' she went on. 'Because I think my vision was meant for you, too.' Then she stretched out her hand.

'Let's go home, Dad,' she said.